The Stagecoach Bride

Sarah Amberson

Published by Trellis Publishing, 2021.

THE STAGECOACH BRIDE

First edition. July 16, 2021.

Copyright © 2021 Sarah Amberson.

ISBN: 979-8223703860

Written by Sarah Amberson.

THE STAGECOACH BRIDE

SARAH AMBERSON

Elizabeth Reed stared out of the stagecoach window. She was heading out west, something that she had only dreamed about for the last several months. She didn't know exactly when she had decided that she was going to choose a life of adventure and danger. Maybe it had been something she always wanted, or maybe it was just a dream that she had created for herself over the past year.

"Are you sure you want to do this? I mean, it's dangerous out west." Her best friend, Hanna's words played back in her mind.

She wanted danger. She was tired of living in her little Chicago town where every single thing was the same every single day for her whole life.

She wanted to give herself a new life, a life of adventure, excitement and newness. The west was the perfect way to do that. Another reason for her leaving Chicago, was the money. She knew that her family had a hard time. She and her three sisters all worked, but still, they struggled to bring in enough money to live well. She wanted to make the load lighter for her family. But she also wanted to find something better for her own future. She didn't want to be stuck in the same place forever.

The stagecoach jolted forward, making her come back to the present. She looked out the window to see the outline of a town. When she had written Aaron Martin, she hadn't expected much. Most of all, she had expected a small explanation, maybe a few letters back and forth.

But she quickly found that she seemed to have a lot in common with Aaron. They liked the same things and they were made from the same cloth so to speak. The more she wrote Aaron, the more she wanted to meet him and if she had to guess, his experience was similar.

He had asked her to marry him only a few months after they started talking to one another through their letters. When the stagecoach pulled into town, she was relieved to see that the town was of a decent size. While she was looking for adventure, she didn't want to be lost in the middle of nowhere with no access to anything. This town appeared to be about perfect.

The stagecoach went down main street, passing a hotel, a blacksmith shop, and a few houses. When it stopped at the stagecoach station, Elizabeth had just gotten curious about the rest of the town. She wondered what Aaron did for a living. He had mentioned that he had enough to support a family, but he had never really wanted to discuss exactly what it was that he did.

She figured that it was because he didn't want anyone to marry him for his money, or maybe he had a different reason. When Elizabeth stepped off the stagecoach, she took in a breath as her eyes met those of a man standing a few feet away.

He had dark hair that fell almost into his eyes. He had stubble on his chin, as if he hadn't shaved for a few days. His shoulders were broad, and he looked like spent a lot of time in the sun. He walked over to her and took off his hat. Now that he was closer, Elizabeth realized that his skin was darker than she realized. It wasn't just because of the sun, it was his natural skin color and it was beautiful.

"You must be Elizabeth." Aaron had a deep voice that made Elizabeth want to hear more.

"That would be me. And I think this goes without saying, but you must be Aaron."

Aaron chuckled. "That is my name. It is a pleasure to meet you Elizabeth. How was your journey?"

"Quite nice, actually, I very much enjoyed the trip. It was a bit long, but it wasn't as terrible as I expected."

"Well, I am glad to hear it. Why don't we go over to the wagon? The justice of the peace isn't far from here. They are expecting us."

Elizabeth nodded, relishing the streak of excitement running through her. Everything was new, the people, the place, the experience. She couldn't wait to get to know everything. This was just what she had wanted.

—-*—-

Aaron couldn't keep from glancing over at Elizabeth. It was still hard for him to believe that such a beautiful young woman would come all the way from Chicago to marry him. She was beautiful and she had the prettiest voice he had ever heard.

He noticed the sparkle in her eye as she took everything in. He had been more than skeptical about finding a good wife through a mail order bride service, despite the fact that more than one person had recommended it to him. He hadn't wanted to risk getting rejected or risk getting a woman who wasn't really interested in a life out west.

"So, I know that we really haven't talked about this in our letters, but I have a ranch," Aaron started out. He hadn't wanted to discuss everything he did in his letters. He felt like it was a conversation that was much better suited to be had in person.

"Really? That sounds lovely. I've worked on ranches on the outskirts of town. I think I can help with the animals, or anything else really. Do you have many animals?" Elizabeth didn't skip a beat and it put Aaron's mind at ease. He had been worried that getting a city woman to marry him would mean he wouldn't have someone who could help him with his new hopes and dreams. But it seemed that Elizabeth was exactly what he needed.

Aaron pulled the wagon to a stop in front of the justice of the peace. Getting married was something he had wanted to do for a long time. It was something that he had thought he wouldn't have the chance to do.

He had tried to find a wife in town, but everyone was either interested in his money, or not the type of woman he was interested in. Aaron got down from the wagon and walked around it, offering his hand to Elizabeth.

"Well, this is it. I know that this is all sort of last minute and might not be what you expected. Are you sure you want to do this? I don't want to push you into anything too fast. I know it's a lot to take in."

Elizabeth nodded. "I am quite sure. I didn't just travel for days so I could get here and turn around."

Aaron hesitated. "You're sure you don't mind being a rancher's wife?"

"Of course, I don't mind. I came here for excitement, adventure and to start my life over. I rather expected it. I believe that it is what I am getting."

"I can't promise much when it comes to excitement and adventure, but there is definitely a new start to be had." Aaron pushed down the voice in his head. He knew that he should talk to Elizabeth about the rest. He knew he should mention that he also wanted a family. He was ready to settle down, to start a slow life. He had spent the past several years growing his businesses and making his finances work for him.

He was ready for a quiet life for a change. Now that he had the money that he needed, he didn't want any more excitement or adventure than the minimum that came with daily life on a ranch. But Elizabeth was willing to work hard. She seemed centered and down to earth and he had come to love the woman he got to know in her letters. Surely, they would figure something out after they were married.

—-*—-

Elizabeth noticed that Aaron was quiet for most of the way home. She hadn't been expecting much, but surprisingly, it was a large cabin with a huge barn, and it was all circulated by fences. There were cows in a pasture by the barn on one side and horses on the other side.

A huge yellow dog came running up to greet them as soon as Aaron pulled the wagon to a halt.

"This is Yella. He's the guardian of the ranch, keeps us safe most of the time." Aaron gave her a grin.

"Really? He looks much too friendly to keep much safe." Elizabeth giggled and tickled the dog behind his ears.

"He really is too friendly." Aaron grinned.

Elizabeth found herself fascinated by the town and by Aaron, but she felt like something was missing. For some reason, she had thought that coming out west would be more exciting. She had imagined that she would meet Indians, and even run across a few robbers or bandits. She would explore places and get to know the world out west.

But from what she could tell so far, she had simply moved from one home to another. Everything that she would see on a ranch back home was on Aaron's ranch. There was the chicken coop, the animals, and the dog, it was all intriguing, but Elizabeth was starting to realize that she might have left one mundane life for another.

"What is the matter?" Aaron asked. He was looking at her with concern in his eyes.

"Nothing, I just... I know that I didn't mention this much, but I thought the west would be very exciting. I thought that it would be different than Chicago. The place does look different, but it is also the same. Does that make sense?"

Aaron sighed. "I know it looks like that, but excitement, it's not really what you want."

"How do you know?"

"Well, excitement isn't always what you might think it will be. Robbers, bandits, storms, things like that... they are scary and life threatening and when you experience them, you'll never want to do it again. The west isn't always the way that it's portrayed in the storybooks." Aaron looked worried and Elizabeth was fairly certain she knew why. He was worried that she wouldn't stick to her end of the bargain. While she was disappointed that the wild west wasn't as wild as she had expected it to be, she was still going to do everything she could to be a good wife for Aaron. She hoped that she would be able to live up to his expectations.

—-*—-

The days passed slowly for Elizabeth. She fell into a routine of getting up, caring for the chickens, making breakfast, and then helping Aaron around the ranch. She tried to make herself content with what she had on the ranch. She tried to forget her dreams of excitement and adventure. But when she closed her eyes at night, that was all she could see.

She didn't bring it up to Aaron. He was a kind man and he was very generous. He had purchased her anything she requested from town. She was a bit surprised that he had the money to do so, but he had insisted that he was more than happy to do so for his wife.

Elizabeth felt bad that she wasn't completely happy with her life on the ranch. She wanted to feel happy and fulfilled with a day of chores and family life, but the more that she did it, the harder it became.

"Elizabeth? Where are you?" Aaron's voice called to her from the front of the ranch. Elizabeth was kneeling in the garden, planting vegetables. She did find that she enjoyed vegetables. She liked feeling of the dirt between her fingers and the little plants slipping into he ground. She loved to see them grow from being almost invisible to being large plants that they could eat.

Elizabeth looked up to find Aaron walking toward her with a crate.

"What is it?" Elizabeth stood and wiped her hands on her apron.

"I got some more chickens. We only have six, I figured a couple dozen of new ones would liven the place right up." Aaron proudly showed her a crate of baby chickens.

"They're lovely." Elizabeth scooped one up, admiring its soft baby fluff before putting it back with its siblings.

"I'm glad you like them. Umm, I wanted to talk to you about something, do you have a moment?"

"What is it?" Elizabeth asked.

"Maybe we could go inside for a while?"

Elizabeth nodded, putting her tools to one side and standing, following Aaron into the house. She watched as he put the crate of chickens down on the porch and then the two of them headed inside and sat down at the kitchen table.

"What is this about?" Elizabeth asked.

"I have something to tell you."

Elizabeth squirmed in her seat. It wasn't like Aaron to speak like he was doing now.

"I know that from the time that you arrived, I haven't spoken much about what I do."

"I just figured that when you were ready, you would tell me." Elizabeth hadn't worried about it too much. While she had come west in partly because she couldn't afford to support herself in Chicago, she didn't care about money.

And as much as she thought that she wouldn't, she'd started to come to care for Aaron, regardless if he had money or not.

"The truth is, I started a bank. I came west, I struck gold, and I started a bank. It's been such a hard few years. I had to deal with a lot of robbers, people wanting to steal what I had worked for. It was maybe exciting but many times it was exhausting and very stressful." Aaron paused and took a deep breath. "I decided that it was time to sell the bank and to start a family. I was ready to live a calmer sort of life and ready to let someone else take the bank over. That is why I put the ad in the newspaper. I just want to know, are you happy here?"

"I don't know. I just...sometimes I think about everything that I could have done or maybe I should have done. My mother used to always tell me that all I would ever amount to was being someone's wife and someone's mother. Maybe that was what drove me to travel west. I felt like I was proving her wrong. But here I am. At least you've accomplished something in your life, something great and impressive." Elizabeth trailed off. She felt so confused and talking to Aaron wasn't helping.

She had thought that she wanted excitement, but hearing that Aaron had gone through the excitement she'd craved had left her feeling a little empty. She didn't know what to think. Maybe she didn't want excitement. Maybe she was just destined to be unhappy for the rest of her life.

"Your life is impressive too, even if you don't think it is. Just being here, out west, it is something amazing. Not many women would be as brave as you. You aren't afraid to work on a ranch. Many women can't live without their tea parties and fancy houses. You can grow plants and food for your household. Not all women know how to do that either."

Elizabeth nodded. Hearing Aaron say that made her think that maybe he was right. She felt a small flame of happiness that he was pleased with her work.

"I should go get the chores in the barn done for the evening, but we can talk again later?"

Elizabeth nodded. She knew that Aaron was probably right. She was most likely allowing herself to get hung up on things that she just hadn't resolved with her past and that was making her look for something impossible rather than what was right in front of her.

Elizabeth shook her head sadly. She wished that she could be sure of herself and proud of her accomplishments, but all she felt was sad.

—-*—-

Elizabeth woke up to the smell of something burning. The smell tickled her nose. She sat up straight in bed. It was past morning. She must have slept in a bit late. Aaron had told her that he wouldn't be home this morning. He had left before sunrise to go into own and get some supplies.

Elizabeth scrambled for her clothes and her boots. She raced to the window and peaked outside.

The barn was burning. Orange flames were curling around the roof of the barn and the sound of horses neighing and pounding on their stalls with their hooves could be heard through the window.

Elizabeth's heart began to pound, and she raced outside. She ran toward the barn, trying to push herself faster. She knew it was a bad idea, but she knew that she couldn't just leave the animals in the barn to die.

When she got to the door, she pulled hard on one side. The first side didn't open, but the second one did open. As she stepped inside, she could see that one of the beams that had been holding up the roof had fallen over one of the doors.

She hurried over it and headed further into the barn. She pulled each stall door open so that the animals could get out, but they balked at the flames. She started with the horse nearest to her, pulling it toward the doorway. It was stubborn at first, but it seemed to realize that she was trying to help. As soon as she'd pushed the first horse out of the barn, she hurried back for the second one.

The barn was full of blinding smoke. It choked Elizabeth, tempting her to go back and rush out the door into the fresh air. But there was only one more horse left. It was one of the young ones, Aaron told her that it still hadn't been properly trained.

Elizabeth heard it's scream as she tried to find it through the smoke. She pushed through the fire, toward the sound of the last horse. It took her a bit longer to open the stall door because she could barely see any longer with the raging fire all around her.

She grabbed the horse's lead and pulled on him to follow her. The horse's eyes rolled back in his head.

"Come on!" Elizabeth called. He reared almost pulling her off her feet. She grabbed an empty feed bag and pushed to up onto the horse's forehead sliding it under the straps of the halter covering his eyes so he couldn't see the flames. She pulled as hard as she could and finally, the last horse followed her. She tried to navigate their way through the rubble, avoiding the worst of the fire, but it was impossible. The section near the door to get outside had been further blocked. There was only a small space left. Just as they got near, the horse jolted past her, pulling the rope from her hands and raced through the entryway.

As Elizabeth tried to follow, a loud crash surrounded her. It took her a moment to realize what had happened. All around her was the sensation of heat and pain. She could hardly think. Another beam had fallen and this time, it had fallen on her leg.

Elizabeth fought tears as she assessed her situation. What if she was about to die?

The thought was sobering, and calming at the same time. She could barely see through the opening of the doorway to the outside where the horses were safe and sound. If only Aaron would come back, maybe he could help her, but there was no guarantee that he was anywhere near.

Elizabeth tried to block out her surroundings. She thought about the conversation she had just had with Aaron the night before. What did excitement matter now? Did it matter that she hadn't traveled, or that she had never gone anywhere to see some grand sight? Did it matter that she hadn't proven her mother wrong?

None of it really mattered. What mattered was that she had come to care for Aaron and now she would possibly never see him again. What mattered was that now she would never know what it was like to be a mother.

She gave a sad smile at the thought. Another loud crash shook the ground beneath her. The barn was falling apart. She could feel it crumbling around her.

She closed her eyes and took herself back to the memory that had changed her thinking so much. Maybe she had misinterpreted that memory. Maybe the words that her mother had told her that day hadn't been understood the way they should have been.

"What about you, Elizabeth? Do you want to live in Chicago when you grow up?"

Elizabeth looked up at her aunt. She had never been asked this question before and she didn't know how to answer it.

"Of course, she wants to live here. This is where her grandparents are from and where we are living." Her mother interrupted before Elizabeth had a chance to answer.

"That doesn't mean that she will want to live her when she grows up. What if she wants to explore? Do you want to go somewhere new?" Her aunt sounded excited at the prospect. At the age of ten, Elizabeth knew little about exploring or going new places and she wasn't sure she wanted to know.

"Elizabeth, child. When you grow up, you will be a mother, and a wife. That is what women do. Do you understand? All the traveling, excitement, the materialistic things, they don't matter to a woman. They are not what is important in life."

Elizabeth brought herself back to the present. She had always taken those words against her mother. She had always thought of it as her mother not believing in her or wanting her to be anything but a mother and a wife. But maybe her mother had been trying to say that what was important was being a mother and a wife. Now that Elizabeth was on the brink of losing everything, she wanted the peaceful calm life that Aaron seemed to crave.

She only wished that she would get the chance to tell him so.

—-*—-

As soon as Aaron rode up to the ranch, he knew something was wrong. He saw the horses loose in front of the house and then he saw the flames eating the barn. He had heard of some people experiencing fires. It was Texas and those sorts of things happened sometimes. But even so, he had never expected for it to happen to him. The first question that came to mind was how the horses got out. His mind went to Elizabeth. Had she gotten them out? If so, where was she?

He leapt down his horse, racing toward the barn. He had a terrible feeling about this situation.

"Elizabeth? Where are you?" he called out.

There was no answer.

"Elizabeth!" Aaron yelled as loudly as he could, searching the ranch with his eyes, hoping to get a glimpse of his wife. Even though they'd only been married for a few short weeks, she had become an important part of his life. He loved her, even before she arrived in town. He couldn't lose her now.

As he got closer to the barn, he saw her. He could just barely make out the bright blue of her dress. It was right there, close to the entrance of the barn, but something was wrong. As he got closer, the heat nearly overwhelmed him. It hit him in waves warning him to stay back and threatening him with harm if he didn't.

He inched his way closer, trying his best to overcome the pain.

"Elizabeth?" he called.

He took off his outer shirt, dipped it in the tank of water that was still sitting outside of the almost nonexistent barn and wrapped it around his face. He then ran head on into the barn. The worst of the heat was as he approached it, but as he passed through the opening, it became slightly cooler.

Elizabeth seemed to be trapped in a spot that was holding the heat away from her at least momentarily.

"Aaron? You're back." Elizabeth's voice was weak, but full of relief.

"Don't worry, we are going to get you out of here."

"It's too heavy. I already tried." Elizabeth's eyes filled with tears. "I'm sorry."

"You have nothing to be sorry for." Aaron tried not to look her in the eyes. He didn't want to face the possibility that maybe he wouldn't be able to get her out of this barn. His eyes landed on the pitchfork. It was within reach.

"I'm sorry for not being more grateful for what we had. I was always thinking about what I could have had and what we could have done. I thought that living on this ranch was boring, but now I see that it was the best thing that I could have ever asked for. Life is more than just about what adventures someone has."

Aaron's heart ached. He didn't want her to be saying any of this. He would rather she find another way to resolve her doubts about their life. He didn't want her to come to harm in order to do so.

"I tried to get the animals out. I didn't want you to lose them."

"You did a great job. They are all safe." Aaron propped the pitchfork against the beam. "This might hurt," he said. He pushed with all of his might, feeling a wave of relief when the beam rolled off of Elizabeth's leg. As soon as she was free, he scooped her up in his arms and went running out of the barn.

As soon as he had stepped away, the entrance crumbled. Aaron laid Elizabeth gently down on the grass a good distance away from the barn. She looked exhausted, but there was a small sooty smile on her face.

"Thank you," she said.

For the first time, Aaron realized how close he had come to almost losing the one good thing in his life. He had lost his parents a good long time ago. He didn't have many friends and he certainly didn't have family. Elizabeth was all he had left. He reached out and cradled her cheek in his hand.

"I almost lost you," he said in a husky whisper.

"But you didn't. We are going to be all right."

"We are going to be all right." Aaron was certain of it. It was going to take them time to rebuild the barn, but the important thing was, they were both alive and well. He couldn't have asked for more.

—-*—-

Elizabeth stared down at the bandages on her hands. She hadn't expected to get out of the fire alive. After they'd managed to catch their breath, Aaron had gone to get help. By the time that others arrived to help them with the fire, it had burned the remnants of the barn all the way into the ground. There was nothing left of the once proud building that had housed their animals.

"Are you all right?" Aaron's voice made Elizabeth look up. He was standing above her with a glass of water. They were in the parlor of the cabin. She had been sitting there since the doctor looked at her hands and bandaged them so they could start healing. In all of her efforts to get the animals out safely, she had burned her hands. Her lungs still burned slightly from all of the smoke she had breathed.

"I think so. Only because of to you. I would have died." Elizabeth quieted at the thought. She still felt as if she were in some sort of dream. The fact that she had come so close to death terrified her.

"I am sorry that I wasn't here. I don't know what started the fire. Maybe it was just the sun hitting a piece of glass right or maybe it was something else. Maybe I left the lantern on when I went in the barn this morning. The thought is haunting me." Aaron looked devastated at the possibility that he might have caused the fire.

Elizabeth reached out and took one of his hands. "It wasn't your fault, Aaron."

"How do you know?"

"I don't, but I do know that this really wasn't anyone's fault. It could have happened for any number of reasons. The important thing is that we are both all right. We can rebuild now. We can move on. We didn't lose anything important. I know that we can rebuild the barn if we work together."

"We can. I am still sorry that you had to go through that." Aaron shook his head. "When I saw you in that barn, when I thought I was going to lose you, I realized how selfish I have been."

"What?"

"I want a calm life, but that is because I already had a lot of experiences in my life. I think it is fair that you have some experiences too."

Elizabeth opened her mouth to protest, but Aaron held up his hand to stop her. "Really, I heard what you said, but you need to listen to me. I realized something while you were in that barn as much as your realized something. I don't have what it takes to become the words greatest adventurer, but if you'd be up to it, we will take one trip a year. I don't know where yet, but somewhere other than here. Even back to Chicago or another city if you like."

"Really?" Elizabeth felt her eyes filling with tears.

"Really. I want you to be happy, Elizabeth, and I know how much you sacrificed when you chose to stay here with me and be my wife no matter what other dreams you had in that beautiful head of yours. This way, we can both get something we want. I can have a peaceful life for most of the year, and I can come with you on your adventure one time a year. How does that sound?"

"I think it sounds pretty wonderful. I love you Aaron Martin."

"I love you too, Elizabeth. I never want to lose you and I am going to do everything in my power to make sure I don't."

Three Months Later

"Where should I put this?" Mrs. Delaney, one of Elizabeth's new friends from town was holding a large pot full of vegetables. They were still steaming and smelled delicious.

Elizabeth moved some of the food on the tables over to make room for the new addition. "Right here is fine. It is almost time to eat."

"Elizabeth, Mrs. Delaney! Come over here, we're about to do the final wall!" Aaron's voice called to them from across the field.

Elizabeth followed Mrs. Delaney as well as all the other women and even the children who rushed over to watch. The men were putting up the final wall of their new barn. It was huge, just like the last one. This one was crafted with love and would always hold memories that Elizabeth wasn't sure if she wanted to forget or cherish. There were still nights where the fire haunted her dreams.

"So, when are you and Aaron leaving for the city?" Mrs. Delaney asked, pulling Elizabeth's attention to her.

"I'm not sure. I think we are planning to go in around two months." Elizabeth's hand went absently to her middle. Her growing stomach was starting to show. She knew from stories she had heard that any day now, she would be able to feel the kicks of their tiny baby in her stomach.

"Are you sure that you can take a trip with the baby?" Mrs. Delaney looked down at where Elizabeth's hand was resting.

"Aaron promised to take it slow. Besides, we aren't really going to the city. Just to the next town over. It is barely a three-hour trip in the wagon."

"That doesn't seem that adventurous." Mrs. Delaney knew about Elizabeth's previous aspirations. Elizabeth had told her many times about the dreams she'd come up with for herself as a child.

"For now, it is as adventurous as I need. Things have definitely changed for me in these past few months."

"I can see that. I like it. You look happy."

"I am." Elizabeth smiled. She meant it, she really was happy.

"Are you ready?" Aaron called. He was with the other men, holding ropes to right the last section of the barn that had been under construction from dawn until now. Aaron had started the construction on his own, but in three months, he'd made very little progress. The people of the town had decided that he needed some help.

Elizabeth wasn't sure how it had started exactly, but before she knew it, there was a date set and then the entire town was showing up at their ranch to help them put the barn up. It had happened quickly, in one day's time.

It was impressive, but it was also touching. It was heartwarming to know that they had a community that cared so much about them that they would come for the entire day and help them in such a way.

Elizabeth watched as the last section of the barn rose to meet the rest. It was a beautiful thing to see the barn standing once more. It made Elizabeth feel like they were actually building together. They were rebuilding and they truly did have everything that mattered. They had love and they had a town that cared for them and they had each other.

"Are you all right?" Aaron's deep voice beside her made her jump. She hadn't even realized that he'd walked over to her, she'd been so busy thinking.

"I am perfect. I am so happy to see the barn up. Aren't you? It's amazing."

"It is." Aaron's face turned somber. "Though I would rather live the rest of my life without a barn than without you. I still think about that day sometimes. I don't know where I would be now if I had lost you." Aaron paused.

"I think about it too, but I use it as a reminder of all the wonderful things I have in my life now. Like you, our baby, this ranch, this life. It is all such a blessing. Sometimes,

I think that life is so busy that we forget everything we have. The fire opened my eyes to what was right in front of me."

Aaron nodded in understanding, then leaned down and placed a gentle kiss on Elizabeth's forehead. He placed one of his hands on her stomach. "How is our little one?"

"He is doing good, I think." Elizabeth smiled down at Aaron's hand.

"How do you know that it is a he?" Aaron's eyebrows rose.

"I don't know, I just feel like it might be."

"Maybe it is a she, or maybe God will bless us with one of each."

"Twins? My goodness, I don't know how we would manage."

Aaron winked. "I think we would do splendidly. Are you excited about our trip?"

"I really think I am." Elizabeth grinned. Even though she had come to love the quiet life she shared with Aaron, there were still tiny fragments of the dreams she'd once thought were the most important things in the world. Traveling was still somewhere deep inside of her, and she was determined that she was going to enjoy the trip with Aaron.

"I am happy that you're excited. Strangely enough, even though I was convinced that traveling was something of my past, I am excited too." Aaron smiled. "I think it is going to be wonderful."

Elizabeth reached down and gave his hand a squeeze. "As long as it will be with you, it is going to be perfect."

Elizabeth meant every word. Maybe the thing that had made her write Aaron in the newspaper hadn't been love, but she had come to love Aaron with all of her heart. She loved the way he treated her. She loved sharing her life with her and she knew that they were going to be happy together for the rest of their lives, as long as they had one another.

THE AMISH LONG WAY ROUND

TERRI DOWNES

Ivy lifted her arms above her head to let Amity help her into her dress. Amity grinned as Ivy's tousled little head reappeared through the neck of the dress. No matter how carefully they brushed and smoothed them, the little girl's curls always bounced determinedly back into place – or out of it.

The patchy clouds covering the morning sky outside shifted, flooding the east-facing room with sunlight. Ivy slipped off the sofa and toddled to the window to peek out at the frosted lawn and copper trees. Amity trailed behind, laughing at Ivy's determination and still trying to fasten her dress.

"Pretty!" exclaimed Ivy, pointing.

Amity ran her hand over Ivy's curls and knelt down for a moment next to her, sharing her view out of the window.

"Yes it is," she said. She leaned over and kissed Ivy's temple. "How did we get here?" she murmured softly. "How did that happen, my darling?"

*****

Beth-Ann Schwartz tumbled out of her sleep, heart pounding. She looked around her in the dark for a moment, wondering what in the world had caused her to wake. But there it was again – yes, someone was knocking on her door.

The knocking began anew by the time she and her husband reached the stairs; it was louder this time, as if the visitor was afraid they might not be heard.

She opened the door to reveal the white face and wide eyes of Amity Weaver. Her *kappe* and hair were wet with falling snow, and a gust of wind seemed to push her through the door as Beth-Ann moved out of the way.

"I'm sorry to wake you," said Amity, her voice sounding oddly raw.

"What is it?"

Amity's words came out in rush. "I was wondering – I remembered – you said you weren't able to make little Mary feed when she came and you had to use that powder stuff, what was it called?"

"Formula?" said Beth-Ann, confused. Amity was not even married, why on earth was she asking about this – unless –

"Do you have any to spare?" Amity choked a little on the question.

Beth-Ann's placed brought a hand to her cheek, aghast.

"Amity – you don't mean – Eliza hasn't – "

Amity nodded jerkily. "We've nothing to feed Ivy with. She's only just four months old, so regular milk won't – "

"Of course."

Beth-Ann fled to her cellar to fetch a spare tin of the formula she had been using for her own little one, pausing for only a moment to shed a few tears for Amity's poor sister – and Eliza's little daughter, and her husband. They were in *Gott's* hands now.

Half an hour later, Amity tried to fight against her shaking legs as she reached her sister's home and heard the sound of Ivy crying. She pushed her way to the kitchen door and almost fell through it, clutching the tin of formula in her hands.

Isaiah stood before the stove. He glanced up, barely, as she entered, then turned his attention directly back to Ivy, squalling in his arms. His eyes were dry, his face pale. As many tears as Amity had shed in the last two hours – had it only been two hours, since Eliza had breathed her last? Could it have been so short a time? – Amity could not help feeling for Isaiah. He looked so young to be a widower. His beard had barely had time to grow.

"Has she been crying long?" she asked, slipping out of her coat and fetching the things Beth-Ann had told her she would need to prepare the formula.

Isaiah shook his head. "Only a few minutes. She slept through everything, I guess. I did wonder if I should have woken her, at the end, to say goodbye, but – " his voice cracked.

"They'll meet again in heaven," Amity said quietly.

As Isaiah hugged his tiny daughter to himself and Amity set to work, she felt a vague realization that she had never really spoken alone with Isaiah before. In fact, she could not fathom why they were alone now. Where was her mother, and her younger sisters? She guessed they were still dealing with their first moments of grief, still sitting with Eliza. She was tempted to go and join them; she knew that she had not yet cried all of the tears that this night would call forth from her.

But no. There was her niece, crying for food, unaware that her mother was gone, and there was Isaiah, far too helpless at nineteen to do any of this alone. The needs of the living would have to come first.

***

It is strange, sometimes, the forms that grief will take. Amity remembered when her father had passed on, how she and Eliza had each crept away to cry at least once a day, and how her mother had forced them to keep up with their chores and keep looking forward. It had been helpful, to have something solid and defined to do.

Yet now, faced with the loss of her eldest daughter, Amity's mother had sunk into apathy. Amity had wondered, on the night of Eliza's passing, how she had been the first to think of what Ivy might need. In the days and weeks that followed, however, she discovered that she was still taking the forefront of such concerns, and could not interest her mother in them.

Her mother did not even want to see Ivy, which just about broke Amity's heart. She understood that Ivy's birth had weakened Eliza to the point where she was not able to recover from her illness, and that it would take her mother a while to get over this – but Ivy's birth had been such a joy to Eliza. She did not regret her daughter, even when she had known she was dying.

Amity shook her head as she stepped through Isaiah's kitchen door. She needed to focus. Isaiah did not have any family who could help him at the moment, and with her mother frozen in sadness, Amity had been coming by every day to take care of Ivy.

She had not spoken about it with Isaiah beforehand; she had simply arrived the morning after Eliza's death and knocked until Isaiah had let her in. She had not been able to think of anything to say to him, and he had clearly not been in favor of small talk either, so Amity had simply gone to work.

After a few days, she had started letting herself in.

Isaiah did all right at fetching his own breakfast and feeding Ivy with the bottles that Amity left every night, but there was no way he could have continued to work and take care of Ivy. He had stayed home, the first few days, sitting quietly and holding Ivy a lot. On the second morning after the funeral, he had headed off to work with nothing but a silent nod at Amity. She had returned it with a small smile of solidarity.

For the past few weeks she had spent her days cleaning, caring for Ivy and making extra bottles for nighttime feeding. In the evenings, she would reheat some of the food that had been left by helpful neighbors and set it out for Isaiah before she left.

Last night, however, had seen the last of the gifted casseroles.

Amity spent the morning wondering what she should do. Isaiah would need to settle on a way to take care of himself. They had not discussed how he might do that – they had not discussed much of anything, except for Ivy's progress at pulling herself into a sitting position unaided.

Was it proper, Amity wondered, to simply take over a man's house? She may have been his wife's sister, but it was not as though she and Isaiah had ever been close friends. He almost seemed as though he did not know she was there, these past few weeks. But she could not imagine what he would have done without her.

And what did it matter if he forgot to thank her? He was not the one Amity was doing any of this for. It was for Ivy – and Eliza – and *Gott,* whom she felt pulling her to this place every morning.

Amity smiled at Ivy, who had pushed herself up onto her elbows on the rug in the living room and was making burbling noises.

"Don't worry, *liebchen,*" she said, sitting down next to her niece. "I won't let your *daed* starve."

If she was looking for appreciation, she found it when Isaiah came home that evening to the scent of her family's secret chicken soup recipe, which Amity presumed Eliza must have made for him at some point. He offered exactly one quarter of a smile.

Amity could not let herself mind, particularly when she saw how big a grin he gave Ivy. She supposed that he had a limited supply of smiles, and had to save them for where they were needed.

*****

Isaiah and Amity had their first full conversation about something other than Ivy exactly two months after Eliza's death. The subject was not by any means interesting, being chiefly about socks, but Amity determined afterward that it had been their first real, friendly interaction. It was about time too, she thought, given that she had all but moved into the man's house.

Admittedly, she might have caught him off guard, having brandished a sock at him from her seat at the kitchen table as he came through the door, demanding to know what exactly he did that caused all these awful tears.

"There's so much darning on this one I'm just about knitting you a new sock!" she had exclaimed.

She had been feeling a little playful, having kept up a running one-sided conversation with Ivy all afternoon, the way she had done with her little sisters when they had been babies.

Isaiah had flushed red – the first color Amity had seen on his face in months – and he had stammered that he had not asked her to mend them, it was very good of her, but it wasn't really –

She had laughed.

"I'm not saying I mind, Isaiah," she had said, waving the sock as she spoke. "I'm just concerned. I mean, it looks as though a bear was gnawing on your foot. Which is considered to be pretty dangerous by most people, you know."

Isaiah had stared at her for a moment and then, quite unexpectedly, chuckled. He was still blushing, but Amity smiled broadly. He reassured her that he had not been fighting with any bears, and laughed quietly again.

Amity was pleased; it was good that he was able to laugh.

After this interaction, Isaiah seemed to awaken somewhat to Amity's presence in his home. And, after a few more weeks, he even went so far as to thank her for everything she was doing for Ivy. He also cottoned on to the fact that the food waiting on the table every evening was no longer the offerings of neighbors but Amity's cooking, over which he was almost effusively grateful. That is, he offered a full third of a smile, said "thank you", and made sure to check that there was enough housekeeping money in the tin.

Amity tried to remember whether he had always been so silent, or whether it had only been since Eliza had gone that he had become like this.

She suspected it was grief that kept him so withdrawn, and so she could not hold it against him. Any time she began to feel a flicker of annoyance over his obtuseness, she would be reminded where it stemmed from, and her anger would float away.

Early on, for instance, she had asked whether she should take care of his laundry as well as Ivy's, seeing as how she was at the house all day anyway. She had not wanted a flood of gratitude, but had certainly been expecting something more than an absent nod of the head.

On venturing upstairs to get the bedsheets, however, she had realized that Isaiah had moved himself and Ivy to a small bedroom at the end of the hall rather than face the room he had shared with Eliza. Amity had wept into the bare mattress of the master bedroom and any thoughts of martyrdom or self righteousness had been washed away in sadness and salt.

And at least Isaiah remained affectionate toward Ivy. Amity had been a nervous to start with, given that her own mother still could not make herself visit this house, that Isaiah might struggle to connect with his little daughter in the face of their loss. But every evening, he proved her fears meaningless when he returned from his work in the fields and insisted on holding and hugging Ivy, having his chance to feed her, and putting her to bed. At Amity's suggestion, he even started talking to her, long quiet rambles about what he had done that day or how much he loved her. His fullest smiles were reserved for when Ivy tried to reply with her strings of strange sounds.

At these moments, Amity was glad that Isaiah seemed still to barely notice her presence. If he had been more aware of her, perhaps he might have become self conscious and waited for her to leave before speaking to Ivy as he did. And those moments that she did manage to witness – they made Amity's day, every time.

***

"I'm headed out, is there anything you need from the store?" Amity called up the stairs.

"Out?" her mother called back. "At this hour? It's barely light – have you finished your *redding*?"

"Yes, *Mamme*. I have to go get more formula, and a few other things."

Amity rubbed her eyes with the back of her hand. It was a little much, handling her chores at home as well as taking care of Isaiah and Ivy. She had not been getting as much sleep as she normally would, perhaps. But it had been more than six months now, and she had settled into a manageable pattern.

Her mother's disapproving face as she descended the stairs, however, suggested that she did not think so well of the system.

"Can't Isaiah get his own groceries?"

"*Mamme,*" Amity said, faintly reproving.

Watching her mother's face flush, Amity knew that deep down the older woman regretted her detachment from her granddaughter and son-in-law. Yet she did not seem to be able to do anything about it.

"I'm just saying," said her mother. "Isaiah's sister said she would be happy to take Ivy in. If he can't take care of her himself then he's no right to ask you – "

"He didn't ask me," said Amity. She wanted to argue that he would have had a right to do so, but she preferred to pick her battles. "And he can't move to all the way out to Pine Corners, *Mamme.* He's still working on Joseph Raber's farm, and Joseph said he might sell him some of his land next year to start his own."

Amity paused for a moment, wondering how she knew this. When had she and Isaiah talked about his work? Sometime last week... they had been talking more, recently, but she had not realized how much.

"He can send her to his sister and stay here," said her mother. "It's not fair to you, or the child – "

"It can't be fair to have his daughter grow up not knowing her father," said Amity, more sharply than she had intended. "Or for him to live without her. She's all he has left – and they won't need me forever."

"And what happens in the meanwhile?" asked her mother insistently. "Are you supposed to keep house for him til Ivy's grown? What about your own courting? You'll be eighteen soon, how are you supposed to settle down when you're taking care of someone else's family?"

Amity looked long and hard at her mother. She could not rebuke her parent – but neither did she want to. Her mother seemed angry, hard, but there was a river or hurt below the surface.

And Amity – she had been hurt, too. But she had had Ivy to care for, and to give all of her love to. She had been able to fill her days with good things, sweet things, and they had soothed her pain. She knew that they had helped Isaiah too, and that every moment spent with Ivy was a reminder of all the good that *Gott* still had for him.

"They are our family, *Mamme*," she said.

Her mother broke eye contact and looked down at her feet.

Then she turned away, unwilling to admit her pain and so unable to have it healed. "Well. I suppose he'll marry again sometime, and you can finally get on with your own life."

Amity nodded at this accession and stepped out into the summer sunrise. As she walked through the humid dawn, however, watching the gold light paint itself onto the undersides of every leaf in the garden, she felt a little sad.

She hesitated for a moment. Surely she was not growing too attached.

It was not her home, after all, her mother was right about that. She did not want to take her sister's place – *Gott* forbid.

She thought about Isaiah for a moment, and how soft he looked when he was with Ivy. How he had started to come out of himself, just a little. How his smiles had become half-way full.

No. Amity drew herself up and clasped her hands. That was not – what this was. This was for Eliza, and for Ivy. Isaiah was a brother. A friend, if he would let himself be one.

Her mother did not need to worry. Amity would just have to be careful.

***

Time was passing too quickly.

It had been doing this for a while.

Isaiah sighed heavily as he wandered down the path which led to his home. He had always heard that time passed more slowly in moments of grief, and that he would feel at the end of each week as though he had lived through a year or more.

But a week after Eliza had died, all he had been able to think was "already?" He had expected that he would have more time, more hours in the day. That he would be able to feel every minute of his grief as it ticked past. As it was, he had barely been able to keep up with everything he had needed to do. It had been difficult, going back to work and leaving Ivy, though spending time with her in the evenings had given him something to look forward to.

And even that – watching Ivy grow and develop – had been going faster. Maybe it was partly due to the lack of sleep; after all, he was not able to ask anyone else to see to Ivy when she woke in the middle of the night demanding to be fed or from teething pains. She already had a few teeth, tiny and perfect just like everything else about her. And she had been pulling herself up on everything she could; it would be only too short a time before she was able to walk unassisted, and before he knew it she would be grown.

And what then? Would time slow once more? Isaiah found himself hoping that it would not. The frenetic pace of his life, the work of caring for Ivy and earning enough to live on, had kept his mind occupied. He had not had to think about what he had lost. He had been able to keep his eyes down.

Away off ahead of him, the sun was beginning to sink rosily toward the hilltops. The evening seemed tinged with gold, the color soaking itself into the thick air. The days were already growing a shorter – this was a fall sunset, if ever he'd seen one, and the air, though muggy, was not holding the heat the way it had been doing the past few weeks. Soon it would winter – a full year since Eliza had gone.

A noise up ahead pulled Isaiah from his dim reverie. It was clear, and light, carrying easily over the garden in front of the house and through the trees toward Isaiah. He recognized it as Amity's voice, wondering for a moment when he had become so familiar with her voice that he could identify it so quickly and over such a distance.

She was standing on the porch, waving at him. She had done that before, he recollected vaguely, back at the start of all of this. Not recently, though. But now – wait.

Why was she doing it now?

For just a second, Isaiah thought that she might have bad news, and a hundred things that might have happened to Ivy flashed before his eyes. His knees locked for a moment, almost causing him to stumble.

But then Amity called again, and he seemed to know her voice well enough by now – again, he was not sure when that had happened – to know that she was happy.

He picked up the pace a little. When he was close enough, Amity shouted across the garden,

"She spoke! Quickly, she said a word, you have to hear!" and disappeared into the house.

Isaiah sprinted the rest of the way to the front door, almost colliding with Amity as she stepped back into the doorway to see where he was.

Amity led him with great ceremony into the front room, where Ivy was sitting on the rug. She picked up her niece and looked at her expectantly.

After a moment, she made a noise of disapproval.

"Come now, *liebchen*, or else your *daed* will think I'm telling tales."

Isaiah wanted to laugh at her comical expression, but was immediately distracted when Ivy pointed downward and said,

"Rug."

Then he did laugh, delightedly, and took Ivy himself so that she could make the demand of him as well.

"Rug, you say? Well, there you go then," he said, setting her down with infinite care.

He sat back in his chair to watch as Amity knelt next to Ivy, pointing at the rug and asking her what it was, clapping every time she got an answer.

As Amity was preparing Ivy's food that evening, Isaiah stayed in the kitchen, trying to get Ivy to repeat her word by pointing at the hearth rug.

"Oh – by the way," he said from his spot on the floor, "Jacob Schwartz was speaking to me earlier. Beth-Ann's brother? He's also working on the Raber farm. He wanted to know if you were going to the Yoder's barn raising next week, I said I'd ask."

He noted that Amity blushed ever so slightly at the sound of Jacob's name. He remembered that the two of them had been courting at some point, and supposed that he should be taking some kind of brotherly interest in such things. Although... he had not really got to know any of Eliza's family that well. He and Eliza had had what was sometimes called a "whirlwind" courtship, and had married as soon as they could. Isaiah had only had a few conversations with Eliza's mother, and had only spoken to Eliza's brothers and sisters about the wedding.

Yet now, as Amity quietly gave him a message in reply, that she would not be able to leave Ivy for so long a time, he felt something tugging at him. She should go, he thought, and enjoy some social time in shared work. Jacob would probably want to invite her for a drive, as well.

"I can stay with her," he said, "it's just for a day. We'd be in a right fine mess if we couldn't keep each other company for a day."

Amity shook her head.

"What, you don't like Jacob?" Isaiah said, smiling, as he remembered the fraught courtships of his older sister.

"No," said Amity slowly, "I mean – I do, but I don't think it's a good idea. Right now. You know, one meeting leads to another, and I don't – have the time."

Isaiah's brows drew together as he followed her meaning.

She was giving up a chance at courtship, he realized. She could not have been for any kind of ride or walk with Jacob, or anyone else, since coming to help with Ivy. She was here most of every day, and then had to go and help at home. This was the time of her life that she should have been seeing to her own future, and here she was, taking care of his.

Isaiah felt the heat of shame across the back of his neck, thinking of how little he had done in return. He felt almost compelled to release Amity from her duties, and encourage her to go to the barn raising and anything else that might be fun and enjoyable for a seventeen year old – eighteen year old? When was her birthday? – but he knew that he was not able to look after Ivy alone, not completely. Not yet.

She was giving him so much. The least he could do was to be her friend in return.

"If you want to go," he said quietly, spreading his hands on the rug "if there's anything of that sort that you want to do, we can make a plan. We'll make it work."

Amity smiled down at him, then pulled a face.

"Well, maybe the fact I'm not so worried about it kind of answers the question in advance, don't you think?"

Isaiah shrugged and smiled a little. "Maybe. You just let me know when it does happen, won't you?"

Amity agreed, though she kept her eyes trained carefully on the stove as she spoke.

Then Ivy finally proclaimed the kitchen rug to also be a "Rug!"

And, after another round of exclamations and excitement, Amity said what Isaiah had spent so long trying not to think:

"I wish Eliza was here. She would have loved this."

Perhaps she knew that he would not be able to reply to this; at any rate, she turned quietly back to the stove as Isaiah caught Ivy up to hug her, burying his face in her soft side.

***

He could not stop thinking about her.

Eliza.

Amity's small comment had not fallen away as the days had progressed, but had instead caught in Isaiah's mind and stayed there, growing and filling his thoughts.

Time had not slowed its pace, but with every step Ivy took or word she spoke, Isaiah increasingly felt the absence of the one he had envisioned sharing these moments with.

He was making more of an effort with Amity, and had found that he enjoyed their conversations even when they weren't centered on his daughter. Yet this almost seemed to make things worse. Every pleasant moment he had, laughing at Ivy or agreeing with one of Amity's funny statements, he would feel a tug of guilt over allowing himself to move on.

This worsened as winter progressed and they began to near the anniversary of Eliza's death. Ivy had started eating solid foods a while ago, but one week before the anniversary Isaiah noticed that she had begun to feed herself with a spoon and a little help from Amity. He looked at his daughter's impossibly tiny hand clutching the utensil, her face a picture of concentration as Amity encouraged her to guide the spoon correctly. Isaiah felt so very, very young and awestruck at the sight, and yet somehow old and weary at the same time. His sorrow had mounted up over the past year, weighing him down until he felt as though he should never be able to stand up straight.

On the night of the anniversary, Amity was quieter than usual. She prepared food for Isaiah as she always did, and got Ivy ready for bed. Isaiah usually put her to bed himself – but this time, as he watched

Amity dress her in her little nightgown, he began to feel a pressure in his chest such as he had not known before.

It was a year. A whole year, without Eliza. And where was he? What did he have? If not for Ivy, would he have anything worth living for at all?

He was barely able to get the words out, but he asked Amity if she would mind tucking Ivy in for him. She had not even replied before he turned and fled to the garden.

He walked swiftly through the sharp air, trying to get away from the house; perhaps trying to leave the pounding of his heart behind him, but it insisted on following. When he reached the dark green vines trailing over the fence at the bottom of the garden, he halted. The fence backed onto a road, and was taller than he was, deeply shaded in the undergrowth and damp with winter rain. He reached out to touch the leaves that covered it, then stepped forward to lean his forehead against the cold surface of the wood.

He was not sure how long he had stood like that when he head a step behind him. He turned and saw Amity – her eyes were wide with concern, her hands held in front of her. She stopped a few feet away, as though she was trying to hold herself back.

Well, of course, thought Isaiah. He was being selfish. Again.

"I'm sorry," he said, choking on the words, "I know, this has to be as hard for you. She was your sister, I don't – I'm not – "

Amity took a small step forward, biting her lip hard.

"You're struggling," she said simply.

Isaiah knew that it was true; Amity had lost the same person as he had, but she seemed to have dealt with it so much better. Was it because she had lost her father in recent years as well? Could one practice, dealing with grief? He should have asked her to give him instructions.

A laugh almost bubbled up at this, but Isaiah held it in, not wanting Amity to think he was losing his mind. Even if he was.

He looked back at the fence.

"This is the ivy?" asked Amity, stepping a little closer, still looking as though she was trying to keep her distance. "Eliza told me about it."

Isaiah nodded. "Yes, I proposed here. My mother was still living in this house, and Eliza and I took a walk in the garden together. We – "

He stopped. Swallowed.

"I never cried," he said.

"What?" said Amity softly, her brows pitching together a little.

"I never cried, Amity, not when it happened, not ever – "

Isaiah felt as though his breath were trying to come out in gasps.

Amity drew her hands in close to herself for a moment. Then she reached out and touched him on the shoulder.

It was too much. And not enough.

Isaiah reached up and grasped her hand, holding it with both of his. She held on in her turn, and he felt himself collapse. His sobs were too strong, to begin with, and Amity held on tight, keeping him steady as if he might have been carried away, as though he could have shaken himself apart. After a few minutes, he grew quieter, his breaths becoming long and ragged.

Somehow their hands ended up pressed against his heart.

***

Isaiah was not sure what to do with himself.

It had been a few months since the anniversary of Eliza's death. He had been feeling lighter, somehow, since that night, perhaps having cried himself empty of everything that he had been carrying around for a year.

He had felt almost dizzy by the time he had finished sobbing so blindly, and had wandered back to the house in a haze before falling asleep on the sofa – so it had only been upon waking that he had suddenly realized what he had done. He had made a point of speaking to Amity that very morning, determined to apologize for touching her, for being so close – not but that they hadn't bumped into each other or brushed hands a hundred times over the past year, but this was different.

Amity had been very gracious about it, saying she understood that grief doesn't make you think straight and that she thought Eliza would have been happy he had had a friend there for him, but Isaiah still felt restless and confused after their conversation. Amity seemed to be as well; at least, she had become very quiet, these days.

Isaiah tried to think about Eliza, but he was finding it more and more difficult to do so after finally managing to express his grief. In fact, he could almost imagine her impatience at him spending all of his thoughts on her when there was a life to be lived.

But what kind of life?

***

Ivy had been measured for new clothes. Amity sat sewing them in the pale spring light, thinking hard. She could hear Isaiah and Ivy in the next room, carrying on one of their nonsense conversations.

Ivy was not just taller, she walking all by herself as well, all over the garden now that the weather was improving. The little thing had fed herself with no help at all, the last week or so. All Amity had been doing was cleaning, some cooking... and anyone could do that. It did not need to be her.

She nodded to herself. It was time, then.

She could not stay here, as she was. The connection she had felt with Isaiah had not been what she had thought – or what she had tricked herself into thinking – that it was.

She could not forget the feeling of their hands together, pressed close. She had prayed to forget it, so very hard, confessing over and over again and asking that her desires be lifted from her – because they were wrong, They had to be. Isaiah had been Eliza's husband. Amity could not love her sister's husband. She could not.

She had not been in love with him, she realized now, back when she had first worried about it. Not yet. The fear had been her heart, maybe, warning her that such a thing was possible. More than possible, that it would be inevitable, given enough time and closeness. And now, here it was.

Amity almost found herself wishing that she believed in ghosts or some such thing, so that she could imagine apologizing to Eliza directly for such a betrayal.

But this was the next best thing. Once Ivy had gone to bed, Amity found Isaiah in the kitchen.

She explained, quietly, that she thought Ivy did not need her quite so much any more, and that she thought it might be time for her to commit to her home duties.

"I'll still help out," she said, scared to look at his face, it looked so disappointed – and she wanted him to look disappointed, which was so very terrible of her – "but I think that my little sisters could take a few turns here and there, and Beth-Ann's offered to come by if we ever needed her. If you ever needed her, I mean."

Isaiah nodded slowly. "Sure," he said. "That makes sense. I'll – we'll miss you round here, of course, but you'd have to move on some time."

His smile was back to a quarter-full.

When had Amity started noticing his smiles, she wondered – had she always done it? Had they always meant as much as they did now? Had she always been so awful?

"Maybe I'll mention this in passing to Jacob," Isaiah joked.

Amity could not help blushing furiously at this reminder of how she should be directing her feelings, and turned away quickly; though in the corner of her eye she could have sworn she saw Isaiah's face fall.

***

Isaiah had thought that he had finally been making some progress with Amity's mother – Amity had convinced her to come and spend some time with her granddaughter a while back. Isaiah still remembered the knowing glances he and Amity had shared when the delighted grandmother had done nothing but gush about Ivy all afternoon, apparently forgetting her months-long reticence to even see the child.

Which was why, upon seeing her frown when she opened her door to find him standing there with Ivy, he felt a mite confused.

"Ivy was missing her aunt," he said by way of explanation for the unannounced visit.

"Tanta!" cried Ivy – her personal name for Amity.

She waved her arms until Amity's mother had stepped aside and Isaiah had set her down, then toddled off into the house at top speed to seek out her beloved.

"Is… Amity here?" said Isaiah awkwardly, thinking that he should have begun with that question.

"Yes," said her mother, turning and leading the way through into the kitchen.

Amity was not in the kitchen, which made Isaiah feel disappointed – and then confused over his disappointment.

"Tea?" Amity's mother offered abruptly, gesturing to the table.

Isaiah thanked her and sat down, although he felt that it would have been somewhat safer to follow his daughter. He wished that he had when he heard Amity's delighted cry from somewhere within the house; Ivy had obviously found her.

"Did you want to speak to Amity?" asked her mother, still with that odd tone.

Isaiah nodded.

He looked out of the window. The summer had filled itself out once more, a testament to the speed at which the world insisted on moving. It had been a few weeks since Isaiah had seen Amity. She had been coming by less and less, and over the past month or so had managed to time most of her visits so that he was out of the house while she was there.

"I know she wanted to move on," he explained, "but I figured that she has to be missing Ivy as much as Ivy's been missing her. Any day Amity hasn't come by, she asks for her Tanta."

"So you were going to ask her to come back?"

"Well, no," said Isaiah, as much as he wished he could do just that. "I know she has other duties here. But I was worried that she was trying too hard, to get us used to the change, maybe, and I wanted to tell her that – that she's always welcome."

He had also been worried that Amity might really have been more uncomfortable than she let on about their encounter in the garden. He figured that maybe they had not talked about it properly; they were friends, after all. He had been too polite in his apology. He should have made her understand how much he respected her, and that he would never touch her when he shouldn't.

Or – ever. He wouldn't touch her ever, that was what he meant. Obviously.

But her mother was still frowning at him. She looked behind her shoulder at the open and empty doorway, then came forward quickly and seated herself opposite him at the table.

"Don't," she said.

Isaiah blinked at her.

"Please don't ask her. You shouldn't." Amity's mother shook her head emphatically. "She's been miserable, Isaiah, and that's a fact. She's only just starting to get over it all, I think, and I don't want her to go back to how she was."

Isaiah stared at the woman across the table.

"Get over it? Get over... what?" he asked.

"All of it, taking care of you both for so long. It took so much of her, Isaiah. Such a big part of her heart she gave to you and Ivy, and I know now that you needed it. But it broke when she had to leave you both, and I don't want to see that happen again."

It... it broke her heart?

No, that was not what she meant. Or, not quite what she meant. Obviously. Isaiah tried to collect his thoughts.

Then a slight movement in the doorway caught his eye.

Amity was standing there, holding Ivy, and judging from the deep red shade spreading across her face, she had heard what her mother had said.

Isaiah took only a moment to understand the significance of her expression. He felt his mouth drop open, just a little, as Amity buried her face in Ivy's side to hide her blush.

The moment seemed to stretch itself out.

"I mean," her mother continued, oblivious, "how is she supposed to get married herself when she's always with you? Is she just supposed to take care of her sister's house forever? What would Eliza say?"

Amity kept her face hidden, looking as though she wanted to run away. Isaiah felt something like a laugh swelling in his chest.

What would Eliza say?

What, indeed?

Isaiah leaned back a little and looked directly at Amity, ignoring her mother's exclamation when she followed his gaze and realized her daughter had overheard her speaking.

"I think Eliza would be pretty happy about it," Isaiah said, hearing his voice stronger and more clear than it had been in a long time. "She always did want the best for the people she loved."

Ivy plucked at her aunt's ear, apparently thinking that something important was going on. Amity's face reappeared, still blushing – but with a look of wonder pushing out her embarrassment and something happy hovering at the corners of her mouth. She pressed her lips together and looked at Isaiah questioningly.

Later, she would tell Isaiah that this was the first time he had ever given her a full smile.

***

"How did we get here, Ivy?" Amity murmured. "How did that happen, my darling?"

Ivy turned toward her Tanta and smiled broadly, reaching out to clutch her hand.

"Pretty," she said – this time, looking at Amity's dress of bridal blue.

"That's a very good question, how *did* we get here?" interrupted a voice from the doorway.

Isaiah was leaning against the door frame, his casual stance belied by the fierce joy in his gaze as he looked at the two beings he loved most in the world.

Amity stood, still holding Ivy's hand.

"The long way round," she said.

AMISH BEAUTIFUL

ELISE FITZPATRICK

Chapter 1 – Hannah Yoder

A cockerel at the corner of the Yoder Farm's courtyard stretched its legs, glanced skyward, and prepared itself to make its customary morning call. The sun was just peaking above the horizon and the dew-covered grass in the meadow swayed gently in the spring breeze.

COCK-A-DOODLE-DOO!!

Already there was plenty of activity on the farm. Two men – one an elder, the other young and beardless – emerged from a shed at the far end of the courtyard, looking tired and unusually disheveled. Last night, a cow had begun to calf but it hadn't been an easy delivery. It took many hours and all of Amos Yoder's skills and knowledge to save both cow and calf but now, *praise be to God*, all was well.

"Come, young Levi," the old man said, slapping the younger's back good-naturedly. "I think I can already smell Martha's coffee."

***

Neither the cockerel's crow nor the men's voices – not even the sweet smell of coffee wafting from the kitchen below – had woken young Hannah Yoder. She was deep in a luxurious sleep, completely involved in her dreams. She had been taking a shoofly pie straight from the oven and placing it on the kitchen table, right in front of an eager ... Levi Hochstetler!

"WAKE UP, SLEEPY!" came the call that shook her from this fantasy. "Get up! Get up! *Redd up!*"

49

It was her younger sister, Ruth Yoder, who was doing the calling, and Hannah knew from experience that if she didn't get up soon she would quickly be contending with some deceptively ferocious blows.

"Ugh, *schweschder*! I'm awake! Can't you see I'm awake?" she said pleadingly, trying to placate her sister. How could Ruth be so chirpy each morning, she wondered, when she could barely lumber to the kitchen in time for coffee?

There was only one year between Hannah and Ruth and truly – though it could be hard to tell for certain some mornings – they were the closest of friends and confidents. And like all close sister-friends, Ruth had a particularly annoying talent of being able to know almost exactly what Hannah was thinking and feeling...

"You were dreaming, sister!" she said suddenly. "What were you dreaming about? Or... *Who* were you dreaming about?"

Hannah tried just about everything in her power to stop herself from blushing, but she could already feel the hot flames of embarrassment rushing to her face.

"Nothing! Nobody! Maybe I was dreaming about the cow!"

Ruth laughed. "Yah, yah! The cow! Come now, Hannah: get washed and dressed; it's long past dawn and I can hear breakfast has started."

Hannah took one last embrace of her warm quilt before reluctantly stumbling out of bed.

***

The kitchen was already full of people and buzzing with early morning chatter by the time Hannah had made herself ready. She walked to her mother by the stove sand gave her a kiss and then to her father at the head of the table, before squeezing herself onto the last available space on one of the two benches. She poured herself some coffee into a pewter mug and stifled a yawn. It was perfect, and the warmth spread through her almost immediately, causing her to smile in contentment.

"Good morning, Hannah." said a voice from across the table. "I trust you had a good sleep?"

She looked up and saw the beaming face of Levi Hochstetler right in front of her. It was a nice face. At least, that's what Hannah thought. He had large hazel eyes which she had noticed sometimes seemed to change color in the sunlight. And his nose: a slight twist in the center from when he'd fallen off an apple tree aged eleven. She felt her face heat up again as she realized she was staring at him still, and that he would – naturally – be expecting some sort of response. Shrugging this awkward pause off as quickly as she could, she desperately tried to suppress any memory of apple trees, shoofly pies or anything from that morning's dream from resurfacing and causing her further embarrassment.

"Very good, thank you." she managed to mumble, before returning her gaze downwards and concentrating very intensely on her mug of coffee. She could feel Ruth's eyes on her; *if she didn't know before*, she thought resolutely, *she knows now.*

"My father has told me the good news, Hannah." he spoke again, seemingly unaware of her embarrassment.

She looked up quizzically. Levi's father was the bishop of this district and, as such, was always first to hear any news. But still, she could hardly think what the bishop and his son had to talk about her...

"Oh?"

"You practice great humility," he laughed. "Isn't it true that you're being promoted to teacher at the school?"

It was true. Hannah had been an assistant at the school for nearly three years, but now that its teacher, Rachel Stoltzfus, was expecting her first baby in the fall, the responsibility for the children's education was to fall to Hannah. It was a great honor and she had even allowed herself to feel a momentary flash of pride when the three elders on the school board informed her of their decision.

"Oh, yah, thank you." she said quickly. She felt strange: her heartbeat had quickened and she was worried it might even burst out of her chest if she wasn't careful. She had talked many times with Levi. In fact, since he had come to work on the farm almost six months ago – toward the end of the last harvest – he had become almost a member of the family. There were few times they didn't share meals with each other, few mornings he didn't wave her goodbye, and few nights he didn't say goodnight. But this time she felt something different. Maybe it was because he had paid her a compliment, or maybe it was because the memory of the dream was still so fresh on her mind.

"I pray that I will be worthy of the position and that I will be able to impart whatever knowledge I possess," she said, considering her words carefully while trying to recompose herself, all the time aware that she sounded quite unnatural.

"God willing!" said Levi. "And maybe tomorrow you will allow me to accompany you to and from church? Then you can tell me more about the school. I confess: it's been so many years since I've been through its doors that you will probably think I'm quite ignorant!"

If every eye at the table had not already been turned their way, they were now, and Hannah knew she must be a bright scarlet color at this stage. Was Levi asking to court her? It sounded like it. She quickly looked toward her father for guidance.

"That is," Levi continued, perhaps noticing the direction of her furtive glance. "If that is alright with you, sir?"

For a moment, her father seemed to be considering him sternly; but when he finally assented, it was in the same jovial voice that was so familiar to them all; "But of course, of course!"

Hannah managed to give a quick smile to Levi, but stared back down at her coffee when from the corner of her eye she saw Ruth give their eldest brother Abram a teasing wink.

Soon the table was chatting as if nothing had passed. But Hannah felt different. She felt scared, nervous and... Excited!

***

"How could you not tell me?!" hissed Ruth when breakfast was over and the two were finally alone.

"Tell you what?" said Hannah. "There was nothing to tell!"

"Humph!" replied her sister, unconvinced.

The sisters were working on a quilt as a present for Rachel Stoltzfus and her new baby. Hannah always found the work therapeutic and it was by far her favorite chore. In fact, she really didn't think of it as a chore at all. Her sister – as was the case with so many things – was the complete opposite. She was all thumbs and hadn't improved much in terms of skill or efficiency since the day she had first picked up a needle all those years ago. But she also enjoyed it as it gave her an opportunity to chat and that was one of *her* favorite pastimes. And ever since Hannah had started working at the school, they had fewer and fewer opportunities to spend time with each other during the day.

"But you must have known he admired you? Even just a little?" she said, taking another moment away from her needlework.

"Levi Hochstetler is a very good, honorable man." said Hannah, diplomatically. "He's been a massive help to our father and I believe he admires all of us greatly."

Ruth looked at her sister in disbelief and said in a good-natured mock sneer, "if he truly does, as you say, 'admire us all so greatly': why don't I join the two of you tomorrow, when he accompanies you to church?"

Hannah couldn't suppress a wide smile from erupting across her face. She had felt embarrassed, shocked but a little gratified this morning at breakfast. Now that she had some time to think it over, her mild gratification at having a man notice her had turned into trilled anticipation and expectation.

Her father had made her a hope chest when she was still a very little girl. It stood at the end of her bed and in it she stored some of her finest pieces of quilt work. One day, she prayed, God willing, she would bring that chest and those prized quilts to her new home to live with the man who would be her husband. This had been her dream for as long as she could remember and those were the thoughts which always flickered across her mind each and every time she passed the smoothly polished and much loved chest. But in these dreams and thoughts, her 'husband' was always incidental to her future. She vaguely hoped he would be an honorable, God-fearing man; someone like her father, perhaps. Maybe he would be tall, hopefully handsome, with a sense of humor, and hard-working. But as to who exactly this man would be, she hadn't thought much about. That was, before Levi.

Levi was the first young man to ever voice any intentions of any kind toward her. She was flattered, of course, but it was more than that: now as she looked down on Rachel Stoltzfus' quilt and thought about her own quilts and her own future, she didn't see a faceless man: she saw Levi, with his wide smile and slightly crooked nose. Was he the one God had sent her? Was he the man she would spend the rest of her life with? With whom she would bring children into the world? Who she was destined to love for all her days?

Ruth had once again taken a momentary pause from her needlework, and was looking at her sister with deep love, feeling an unexpected wave of joy. It was true that she loved light-hearted gossip but at her very core she was a warm and generous girl. Looking at her elder sister in that moment she could see: Hannah was truly in love, and Ruth had no intention of waking her from her affection-filled reveries.

She sighed deeply, looking at her section of the quilt and noticing absent-mindedly a small error that would need to be picked out and fixed. She hoped that she would one day soon feel how Hannah felt, and that she too would find a man who would love her and cherish her and make her aimlessly stare into the distance, as her sister was now.

But, she thought with regretful resignation, she would have to find a man who could overlook her quilting...

Chapter 2 – Elam Lapp

Tall, handsome and with thick strawberry blond curls which struggled to be contained under his wide-brimmed hat, Elam Lapp struck a striking figure. Aged twenty-two, he also stood out favorably from the rest of his peers because he seemed relatively exotic and was a breath of fresh to the admiring Holmes County youths. He himself hailed from Lancaster County, but had, over the years, come to spend a great deal of his time with his maternal relations in Ohio. His mother had died shortly after his birth and though his father had remarried a kind, caring woman who became and remained his much loved Maemm, he frequently felt disconnected and on the periphery of his family and community.

His mother's people, the Hochstetlers, had been his saviors. His connection to them had always seemed so natural, and it gave him immense joy to be able to feel that he knew his birth mother through them. His uncle was the bishop of these parts and had become a valued teacher as well as someone for whom he felt great love. And then there was Levi. Although all the Hochstetler children held a place in his heart, it was for his cousin, Levi, that he felt the greatest and most enduring link. They were close in age, close in temperament, and – as children – close in mischief-making. In fact, it had been Elam who had persuaded his cousin to climb that ill-fated apple tree all those years ago, and it was he who had concocted a cover story for Levi's broken nose.

In spite of the uncertainty Elam frequently felt about his place and purpose in life, his faith in God was unwavering. Even in his darkest hours, he trusted his life into His hands; nothing felt more natural or right to him than that. Yet, today, he couldn't suppress a creeping feeling of anxiety. He knew that his cousin was suffering and that all those things that seemed to come so natural and right to him did not come so easily for Levi: for a long time he had been struggling with his relationship with God and this had caused a strain in his relationship with his father, the bishop. That was the main reason, Elam was sure, for Levi choosing to work and spend so much time at the Yoder Farm: his cousin was finding his own home too stifling to get his head and heart in order.

Elam knew what a good person Levi was – better than him, he often thought – and he knew he would make a fine, honorable man. But if his cousin couldn't find resolution in God, where would he find solace? Where would he find community and family? Where would he find love?

He wasn't being entirely selfless in his anxieties: he feared what the loss of his cousin would do to him, and how he would manage to navigate through life without his best friend by his side.

Chapter 3 - Levi Hochstetler

Levi let a massive yawn escape his body as he stretched his arms out wide. He loved working with animals and the calving season was by far his favorite time of year. Most other people liked the end of the harvest best of all, but not him. The end of the harvest marked the beginning of the celery crop, which itself marked the commencing wedding season and all the festivities associated with it. It wasn't that Levi didn't enjoying being with other people – far from it – or that he grudged other people their happiness. No, what did concern him, though, was that his own discontentment and fears could infect those around him: good people, people he loved.

But out here in the meadows he felt free of all such worries. He loved his cows, and come wind, rain or shine, he was happy to be out here with them. Strictly speaking, of course, they were Amos Yoder's cows, but Levi knew each one by name and temperament. He had been there at each birth this year and, *Gotte Wille*, he would be there for each of the ones to come.

He yawned again. He had had barely any sleep last night and this morning's coffee at breakfast seemed a painfully long time ago. He walked over to a young heifer and gently scratched her ear, suddenly smiling to himself: thinking of breakfast had reminded him of Hannah Yoder.

He had felt a need to escape his father's house. His faith and commitment to the community had troubled him for some time, but he wasn't yet willing to make such a life-changing decision as to leave everything he'd ever known behind him forever. And so he chose to work for the Amos Yoder. The Elder had needed another strong pair of hands to work the farm and being away from his father for most of the week gave Levi the separation he needed to think through his life and choices.

He came to the Yoder's to find the courage to make a decision: a decision to leave. But instead he found something quite unexpected: a reason to stay. He found Hannah.

Of course, Levi had known Hannah her entire life, but always from afar. He knew her as Hannah the little Yoder girl, or later as a Hannah the assistant at the school; never as Hannah the young woman, and certaily never as Hannah, a young woman who could become his wife.

But something happened that first night he had had dinner at the Yoder's. A timid smile or a pinking of her cheeks which stirred something in his heart he couldn't explain. As those first days turned into weeks, he learned her laugh and saw how she scrunched her nose when she was trying to concentrate hard on a piece of work or a page of a book. She was shy and often quite reserved, but humorously competitive when the household gathered to play board games. She was above all else a kind, gentle soul. But, and he smiled again as he thought of this, even her flaws brought him joy: each morning without fail she would emerge from the upstairs rooms, flustered, irritable and ever so slightly bedraggled. It amused him because after her morning coffee she instantly transformed into the perfect Hannah that the whole community knew and loved.

And there was that word: love. He had tried so long not to say it, even to himself, but he couldn't suppress it any longer: he loved

Hannah Yoder. He wanted her to be his wife. He wanted to love her and cherish her for all of their earthly days.

The heifer shook her large head, waking the young man from his thoughts and take notice of his surroundings. Walking toward him now was a young man. It was his friend and cousin, Elam. Levi smiled once more: he would tell him everything and they would rejoice together.

***

After Levi had finished telling his cousin all about Hannah – her perfections and adorable flaws – and how today at breakfast he had taken the first step in courting her formally, he waited for his reaction. It was, however, slow in coming and not quite what he'd expected.

"I think," began Elam. "I must have met her many times before. But it's been some years since I've visited you and all I can remember of Hannah Yoder is a young, gangly, serious girl."

"Yah, yah," interjected Levi, who was feeling slightly defensive. "She is quite different now. Well, no. She is still quite serious ... with people she doesn't know too well, that is. Once you get to know her she is funny and sweet in equal measure. And yes, she is still young. But now she is a young woman and not a young girl. But gangly? No! She is really quite graceful ... as long as it's not first thing in the morning."

Elam gave a weak smile, "You sound happy and she sounds wonderful."

"But?" said Levi. "I feel like there is a 'but' coming!"

"If this is your choice," said Elam. "Then truly I'm happy for you. More than that: I am happy for me too. You know I consider you more of a brother than as a cousin, and if by this choice it means that you'll stay within our community then that means not only do I get to keep you as a brother, close by my side, but that I also gain a sister. This would be the best possible result for me and I will rejoice forever if it is the best possible result for you too. But is it?"

Levi said nothing. He hadn't an answer to give. Not an adequate one, anyway. No one knew better than Elam the conflict Levi had in his heart. He had spent part of his *rumspringa* in Lancaster County with his cousin and family and it was during that time that his relationship with Elam had gone from that of mischievous youths to one of deep, fraternal trust and respect. Elam had been the first person Levi had confided in that he was filled with doubts, and it was Elam who had convinced him not to make any immediate or rash decisions.

"Consider, my dear, dear friend," Elam continued with a note of desperate pleading in his voice. "What damage you might do if you encourage this girl – a girl you say is good and kind and gentle – to give you her heart, when you don't even know yourself where your heart lies. If you court her, and fall in love with her and marry her, what will you do if in twelve months or even in twelve years you decide you want to leave? Will you make her leave also? Or will you grudgingly stay against your own wishes and desires?"

Levi felt devastated. Elam hadn't said a single word which he himself hadn't thought many times before, but it seemed so much more real and earth-shattering when it was said out loud and by someone else.

"You're right..." he heard himself say, desperately wishing the words coming from his mouth weren't true. He wondered if he should go to Amos Yoder straight away and tell him he had to leave, for good. Should he go to Hannah? Or would that just cause more harm?

Elam looked at his cousin in pity, taking him by the shoulders and embracing him with all the fraternal comfort he could muster, saying, "my cousin, my brother, my friend: don't despair. We'll pray that you get your answer, and I will pray in particular that Hannah *is* your answer. In the meantime, can't you still look forward to accompanying her to church? And after there will be a *sing*, or so I'm told. I will have a chance to meet her and see all of her wonderful qualities for myself!"

Levi gave his cousin a half-hearted smile. Barely an hour previous, he had felt so alive and happy and now he felt more confusion and unhappiness that he had ever felt before. He would still bring Hannah to church tomorrow, and he would still talk to her and be convivial to her at the *sing*, but Elam was right: he couldn't give her his heart until he knew exactly what his own contained.

Chapter 4 – Hannah Yoder

Hannah didn't see Levi again all the rest of that day, and he wasn't back in time for dinner or prayers. But this wasn't all too uncommon, especially at this busy time of the year and she went to sleep that night wrapped in a warm blanket of joy and in sweet anticipation for all that the next day was sure to bring.

Church always began early – early, that is, for someone like Hannah – and this week it would be taking place in the Raber's home, some twenty-five minutes away by buggy from the Yoder Farm. Somewhat miraculously, Hannah was awake before Ruth even had the chance to come over and shake her from her usually deep slumber. She was extremely excited, and could barely hide it. She had spent the night dreaming of Levi and this morning she wasn't ashamed of it. All the things that she had previously thought were 'pleasant' about Levi had now been elevated to 'perfections' and everything she used to 'like' she now 'loved'.

She and her sister bathed and dressed, and then began to pin each other's hair. For a moment, Hannah's gaze lingered over her reflection in the small mirror above their wash basin. She appraised herself with new eyes, before averting them with a slight pang of guilt. She had never been prideful about her appearance or covetous about others, but she now had a deep desire to know how she looked and how she compared to other girls Levi had seen. He had been much further away from Holmes County than she ever had and seen more girls, both Amish and English, than she had boys. She casually wondered what it would feel like to wear the makeup that some of the English girls wore, and then panicked, wondering whether Levi would like her better or worse if she looked more like them.

Her sister grabbed her hand and squeezed it before kissing her softly on her cheek.

"Come," she said. "Let's get a cup of coffee before we have to leave."

***

Levi had evidently not stayed on the farm the night before as he wasn't at the table when the two girls came downstairs, but Hannah remembered that he had probably had to return to his father's house to collect his buggy. And, she thought in a moment of delight, he would need to tell his father, the bishop, of his intentions to accompany a girl to church.

For the second morning in a row, Hannah felt all eyes were on her. But today she neither blushed nor felt any embarrassment. She simply smiled at each of them in turn in wordless recognition of the momentous nature of the day.

Shortly after 7.15, they heard the distinctive sound of a buggy approaching. It took just about every iota of self-control for Hannah not to jump up and run outside to greet *her* Levi, but somehow, amazing even herself, she managed it.

"Come!" her father said to the table at large. "Let's be off." He kissed each of his children in turn as they filed out the door, taking a second longer over his eldest daughter.

"*Gute mariye*!" came the voice awaiting them outside. Levi looked just as happy as he had when Hannah last saw him the day before and, she thought, just as handsome. She beamed at him as he and her father exchanged pleasantries; she was truly very happy. She began making her way toward his buggy when he spoke again.

"Since there is plenty of room with me," he said, just as cheerfully as before. "Had I better not take Ruth with me also?"

Hannah stared at him in shocked disbelief. She imagined Ruth was doing so too. It was not as if they hadn't ridden with him to church together before, often with a gaggle of the younger children, but wasn't the whole point of this morning that it would be just the two of them?! She was confused and hurt, and she began to feel the heat return to her face.

"There's no need," said Amos Yoder, who was evidently slightly perplexed by the situation, but was also old enough and wise enough to know that the situation should be defused gently. "Ruth will be quite happy with us, I think."

"Yah!" said Ruth, a little too eagerly. "After all Maemm will need me to hold Jakob."

Hannah was beginning to feel angry, an emotion she very rarely felt. She didn't want to be standing in the yard debating where Ruth should sit, with her whole family as witnesses. She was meant to be in the buggy with Levi. They were meant to talk, to chat, to court, and to fall completely and utterly in love. She had spent the whole of the last day and night building up a fantasy in which he had the central role. Now she had no idea whether what to feel or what to think. She grabbed her sister's hand, feeling a pang of jealousy and said shortly, "come on, we'll be late if we don't leave soon."

With the initiative taken, Levi and the rest of the family climbed into their respective seats in awkward silence.

Chapter 5 – Ruth Yoder

Levi maintained polite conversation throughout the journey and tried asking Hannah a number of questions about her new role as teacher, and about her hopes for the school. Hannah, for her part, kept the responses as brief as possible without being overly cold or distant. And Ruth sat awkwardly as a buffer between the two, quite unsure about why she was even in this situation.

When they reached the Raber's homestead they alighted and thanked Levi with all the proper decorum expected before joining their parents and the rest of their family in silence. Ruth wanted to grab her sister's hand, to hug her and to take her aside and talk to her, but surrounded by their entire parish, she was unable to do any of that. She tried to brush her hand against that of her sister, but Hannah quickly pulled hers away.

She felt utterly forlorn and guilty. She knew she hadn't done anything wrong, but it felt as though she had, and it felt as though Hannah thought so too. She tried to lose herself in the prayers and hung onto every word the bishop uttered as he walked to and from the two large rooms in which they were gathered, but it was all in vain: she still felt miserable.

Her mind kept wandering and she worried about what would happen after church was finished. Her oldest brother, Abram, Hannah and she were all meant to stay at the Raber's for the weekly *sing* – the main social event for the youth in the parish. But would Hannah insist on leaving? Would Levi stay?

Feeling a burning tear in the corner of her eye, she opened up her bible and began staring at the printed words, desperate for any encouragement or solace.

***

It was a beautiful day: the first proper warm rays of sunshine of the year, and most of the youths who were old enough were looking forward to hours of revelry and enjoyment. Ruth stuck close to her sister who seemed to be stubbornly making a point of staying for the games and *sing*. Ruth had never known Hannah to have a drop of malice or vindictiveness in her, but she could tell that she was just hurt enough to want to pretend to have a wonderful day and make sure Levi saw her having a wonderful day.

She saw Levi approach them, accompanied by their brother and a tall, handsome young man Ruth vaguely remembered as being one of the Hochstetler's out-of-town relatives.

"Hello!" said Levi, slightly less chirpily than before. "You all know Elam, yah? My cousin and the very best of friends."

After making their salutations, they walked together to a large stretch of tightly cropped grass set aside for the day for volleyball. Ruth loved playing, but she thought it might be her duty today to stay beside Hannah until she was definitely shooed away. Levi walked ahead with Abram and the pair spoke animatedly, while Elam held back a few strides and worked with the sisters.

"I've been hearing many things about you recently," he said, before quickly adding, "all good, of course!"

Hannah laughed and Ruth was pleased to hear that it was genuine.

"It's been nearly three years since I last had a chance to visit my family here, and you have changed very much in those years!" he said. "Both of you, that is."

It was Ruth's turn to blush now.

"You like it here?" she asked feebly.

"Like it?" her replied. "I love it! Maybe one day, I'll stay forever!"

She blushed a little more and before she even knew what she was thinking she blurted: "you really should!"

Hannah looked at her younger sister in amazement. She had never seen her blush in her life. Ruth was always so self-assured and gregarious. But it wasn't just Ruth who felt Elam's magnetism. He had a way about him which made you feel almost instantly at ease with his presence. By the end of the first game, the two girls each felt that he was a good friend and were as comfortable with him as they might be with a cousin or close family friend.

Ruth could see that her sister was enjoying his company just as much as she did. She felt an emotion rising in her chest that she didn't instantly recognize or like. It just didn't seem fair that her sister should have the attentions of two men, even if she was the eldest. Although, she thought, trying to be conciliatory: perhaps Hannah no longer had the attention of one of them?

Later that evening, however, Ruth observed that that was not the case. The three of them had made their way indoors to join in in the singing. She happened to look over her shoulder and saw Levi: his face filled with longing, sadness and jealousy.

Chapter 6 – Hannah Yoder

For a number of weeks, Levi seemed to keep his distance from Hannah. He was polite, and friendly, but he didn't ask for any private moments of her time or ask to accompany her to any more *sings* or socials. Truthfully, had he asked, she very probably would have said no.

At first she had felt humiliated, but that had subsided and now all she felt was empty. It had been 24 hours of pure joy, that was all, followed by weeks of pain. Because, as much as she tried to convince herself to the contrary, she could never look at Levi again without seeing the man she thought she'd loved and the man she thought had loved her back. She kept herself occupied with her chores and her work at the school, and tried not to let anyone else around her see that she was hurting.

Both she and Ruth had seen a great deal more of Elam over the past weeks, and those moments were the only ones of levity left in her days. They of course saw him at church and at socials, but he began calling to the house on pretext of seeing Levi. Hannah had her doubts. Did he like her? It seemed so, but then he seemed to like everyone, including Ruth. And how did she feel about him? That might be even more difficult to answer...

With Elam, she felt a great fondness, but there was always an invisible wall that seemed to separate them. She knew what it was too: it was Levi. She felt it was too soon to feel anything for anyone. She even wondered if she would ever feel the same way again about anyone, or would every meeting from now on be tainted by the memory of Levi?

The quilt for Rachel Stoltzfus was nearly complete. She had had to redo one or two parts where Ruth had done a less than stellar job, but it was a beautiful creation. She looked at it longingly and considered its significance. Was it ironic, she wondered, that they were asked from a young age to shun individualism, vanity and lavishness, when they then created such magnificent and valued objects? And in her own life, was she wrong to want love? Was it wrong to demand God to give her a man to hold her and care for her?

For the first time in her short life, Hannah felt alone.

Chapter 7 – Elam Lapp

For Elam, the last few weeks had been some of the best and the worst of his life. They had been the best because he had rarely felt so at home. He felt valued and an integral part of the community, and he loved his new place in it. He really didn't want to leave.

And then there were the Yoders. Levi had been right: Hannah was special. Her shy nature made every hard-earned smile and ring of laughter all the more pleasurable to witness. He kept finding excuses to return to the farm: messages, deliveries, 'urgent talks' with his cousin. He would always be invited to stay for dinner, and then maybe a board game or an evening of stories and songs.

As each of these evenings passed, Elam felt his admiration for Hannah grow, and as his fondness grew, so did his feelings of guilt and treachery. That was why these weeks had also been some of the worst in his memory. A choice lay ahead of him: profess his love for Hannah and risk losing his best friend, or say nothing and risk not ever feeling like he belonged again.

He already regretted coming down quite so hard on Levi that day in the meadow, though he didn't regret having said something: Hannah was too precious a person to allow be hurt. But had he been speaking the truth before? He had said we would be happy for Levi if Hannah was truly the one for him, and that he would be overjoyed to have gained a sister. But now that he knew Hannah, would he be satisfied by that?

He spent his evenings with the Yoders, but he spent his nights praying for guidance.

Chapter 8 - Levi Hochstetler

Much of Levi's nights had been spent in prayer also. He knew Elam had been right in all the things he had said, but it tore him up inside that the only person in the world he truly loved now probably hated him.

After that now infamous morning when he had refused to be alone with Hannah, he had tried to make retribution, but she no longer seemed interested in him. He understood why and though it hurt him, he couldn't grudge her. But what of his best friend, Elam? It was transparently clear that he had an interest in Hannah, but had Levi any right to complain or feel sore by his actions? And, after all, were he to leave his community and religion, would it maybe not be a good thing for the two people he loved best to find solace with each other?

His head said yes, but his heart said no.

He had kept his distance, but he was never too far away. He needed to be close to Hannah, to her kindness and to her love. Those few words they exchanged or an off-guarded smile were all that now sustained him. One day, though, he was nearly reduced to tears when he observed her working on a beautifully crafted quilt. It set his mind racing: a home, a wife, a family; all the things he wanted. And Hannah, the person he wanted those things with.

But what about God? Where was God in his life?

One evening, he sat balanced on the meadow's fence, staring out over the field where the cows grazed contentedly as their calves played and frolicked between their mother's legs. Elam joined him, climbing onto the fence to settle into the discussion each knew was coming, but which both had been putting off.

"You know," Elam began. "I told you I just wanted you to be happy. Nothing in that has changed. I told you I wanted you to know what you wanted in your own heart before you went messing with anyone else's."

"Yah," his cousin nodded. "It was hard to hear, but you were right."

"Maybe," Elam continued. "But maybe I should have taken some of my own advice. I have always been comfortable with my faith, but that doesn't mean I've always known for sure my place in life. But I think I know now: my place is here in this parish. *Gotte Wille*, I will find a wife who will put up with me! But even if I don't, my place is here. And so is yours."

"I wish I had your confidence, but my faith isn't as strong as yours."

"No," said Elam. "But your love is."

They sat in silence for some moments before Elam once again spoke,

"But perhaps you'll give me some advice? I wish to approach Amos Yoder to ask him if I might be allowed bring his daughter out for a walk? You have experience in that field, no?"

Levi stared up at him in confusion.

"Ruth." said his cousin, laughing. "I want to ask Amos Yoder if I can bring Ruth for a walk."

Levi exhaled heavily in relief before breaking out in a smile, "Ruth? Yes, I will help you win her over!"

***

The quilt was finished: every panel straight, every stitch in place. Hannah smoothed it out and felt it admiringly. She was so absorbed that she didn't notice Levi entering the room. When she did, she kept herself composed.

"Hello," she said. "I'm just putting away Rachel's quilt. The baby will be born any week now, and-"

"I wanted to talk to you. Alone."

"Oh?" she said, trying to sound only vaguely interested.

"Yes. And to apologize."

"I don't think-"

'Please!" he interrupted her again, pleadingly. "Please listen to me."

She finished folding the quilt, sat on the couch, laying her hands on her lap.

"I've treated you badly, worse than I've ever treated anyone. But please try and believe me: I did it out of love, and because I thought – wrongly – it was the only way to protect you."

"Out of... 'love'?" Hannah stammered.

"Yes, my dearest." he said, coming close to her, kneeling beside her seated form, and taking one of her hands tenderly into his. "Out of love."

"For much of my life I have found myself questioning my faith and refusing to put my faith in God. I have asked Him to show me love, and when I thought He didn't answer, I became angry at Him. But now I see what a fool I was. He did show me love, because He showed me you."

Hannah felt her eyes fill with warm, joyful tears.

"I've wandered from His path often, and I feared to take your hand in case I led you astray also."

"But you're not worried about that now?" she asked.

"I am weak, but God knows that. That is why He sent me someone good and loving and strong. With my hand in yours, I will follow you on His path, no matter where it leads. I have no fear of my surrendering my life and will to Him because," he took up the hand he held and brought it to his lips. "He has truly given me every blessing in return."

Tears rolled down Hannah's face, but love still shone through it. Levi was quite certain: even with tears that rolled down her cheeks, none was quite as beautiful as hers.

THE AMISH TREASURE

MARISA MEYER

Chapter 1

The air was clean and smog free and for a moment Caylee wanted to go all Titanic and spread her arms and raise her nose to the air as she sat in one of the buggies she hired from Ed's buggies.

"So, you're visiting family?" Sam, the driver asked curiously.

"Not family, just acquaintances," she smiled, "Does Strasburg get a lot of visitors?"

"O' ya, we have tourists that come throughout the year," he said and pointed across to cemetery across the open field, "That there, is the most popular place. People come here to see the ghosts."

"I've heard about that," Caylee said as she studied the cemetery from a distance.

"Ya, it's the whispers and strange noises, but even better is Gondor Mansion, where they say the spirit of Annie lurks at night," he shrugged, "but I have never seen her."

Caylee laughed and shrugged one shoulder, "I guess everyone wants to believe in something."

"Ya, das gud, but believing in the wrong things can bring more harm than good."

"And what is it that you believe?"

Sam looked at her with amusement etched on his face, "Well I'm Amish, I believe the bible."

"That's true," she smiled and then sat back and took in the scenery as they rode further into Strasburg. No-one but the Fisher family knew why she was really here, and they agreed that she wouldn't tell a soul. Was it not for Ella, the eldest of the siblings who convinced her father to allow her to come to their home and get up close and personal to with the Amish village and the stories that surrounded the hauntings of Gonder Mansion, she wouldn't have anything to write about.

She had met Ella a few years before, when she came to Philadelphia for her Rumspringa, and it was pure chance. Ella had found herself in quite a predicament when she had gotten a little tipsy at a local hangout with a few other Amish friends, and a cowardly brute tried his luck with the innocent girl. Caylee had taken it upon herself to step in and save the day and since then they have been the best of friends. In fact, it had been Ella's idea in the first place to invite Caylee to visit. At first she wasn't too interested, after all, what more could be said about the Amish, that hasn't already been covered by Amish converts and those who claim to have fled a cult. But when she did her own research into Strasburg one thing stood out, the so called hauntings and that had been enough inspiration for her to pack her bags and pay her friend a visit.

Being a freelance journalist had its benefits, she could tell just about any story she wanted to without a glorified editor trying to tell her otherwise. If she wanted to write about the enigmatic taste of peanut-butter-banana-flavored ice-cream, she could just as she could do an entire blog on whether or not water is wet.

But even more so, doing a story on the mysterious hauntings in the village after dark gave her the escape she so much needed. She had done the one thing she thought she would never do. The very thing she fought so hard against, but in the situation she found herself in at the time, she saw no other way out. And although her secret is safe with her, this time away from society and the reminders of what she did might just give her the reprieve she needed, and what better way than to write about someone else's misfortune.

Her luggage, which wasn't really much, was stacked on the luggage rack and tied down with multiple ropes to keep it from falling off, but she had insisted on entering the small Amish village of Strasburg as modestly as she could. She even ordered a few items of Amish clothing online in order to fit in as best she could.

White farmhouses stood scattered across the landscape like patches of snow surrounded by fields of corn and pastures of green grass, and it felt as if she was entering a linear time dimension from the past. They passed the big barn with the words The Amish Village painted on the front wall, and Sam turned left down a dirt road that led into the small town. Suddenly it was as if the place had come to life. Women and children walking with a slight skip in their step, men working in the fields or busy doing carpentry on the side of the road was the first thing that impressed her. They all seemed so happy and carefree, especially the children, the atmosphere of this place was contagiously joyful.

"Oooi!!" Sam called as he pulled on the reins and the horses drew to a stop.

The house was old but well looked after, white walls with black tresses and a door dead center with four square windows on either side. It was a modest house, but the garden around the house was magical. Yellow and white daisies bloomed brightly in front of the house along the small stone path that lead up to the narrow porch. Caylee had to smile, it was exactly as Ella painted it.

"Caylee!" a familiar voice sounded from behind her and before she could say a word, Ella flung her arms around her shoulders.

"Hey Ella!" she laughed and hugged her friend.

"I'm so glad you came, Daed and Mamm is so excited to finally meet you, they have prepared a wonderful welcoming meal," she babbled on.

"Well I'm looking forward to it," she smiled, "But first I need to get settled in and just change my clothes."

"Of course you do, I have some dresses if you want to try them on?"

Caylee smiled and took her luggage from Sam and paid him for the ride, "Thank you Sam."

"Enjoy your stay," he grinned and then left.

Ella grabbed Caylee's bag and rushed up to the door, "Come, I'll introduce you to the family."

Suddenly Caylee felt nervous, although she opted for something modest to wear, she was worried that the green dress complemented her physical appearance too much. She knew that the Amish were big on not drawing attention and fashionable styles were on their big no-no list and anything that drew attention to the individual signified pride, which was in direct disobedience to God. She tucked the loose strands of her red hair behind her ears and ironed down her green dress that reached just below her knees and took a deep breath before entering the house.

"Everyone, this is my friend Caylee," Ella said excitedly and then turned to her, "Caylee, this is my family. My mom Mary, my dad Abram and," she paused and looked around, "where is Caleb?"

"Welcome to our home Caylee," Ella's mother smiled and gave her a hug, ignoring her daughter's question.

"Thank you Mrs. Fisher," she said, "I really appreciate the fact that you've invited me into your home."

Ella had told her about her family and warned her about Caleb, her older brother who happened to be completely opposed to the idea of having a journalist sneaking around the town, so she fully grasped Ella's mother's evasion of the issue.

"Welcome," her dad simply said, and although his lips didn't even twitch into a welcoming smile, there was something warm and comforting about him.

She smiled and extended her hand, "I'm a woman of my word Mr Fisher, and I promised Ella that I won't take any photos of anyone in the community," she reassured him.

"I believe you," he said and then gestured with his head, "Come, dinner is ready."

Surprised that they are having dinner so early, Caylee followed the rest though to the dining room, a quaint cozy area that reminded her of her grandmother's kitchen where she used to visit so often as a kid and she instantly felt at home.

Chapter 2

At dawn the soft humming of the wind that whistled through the trees during the night had become a fierce rustling and rain slanted against the windows sending a cold shiver through Caylee. If she had it her way, she would just stay here, curled up in bed, but she couldn't dare to go back to sleep, not with the dreams that plagued her. It was always the same dream. A little infant dressed in a pink onesie, sleeping peacefully in a meadow, but then it changes and dark faceless creatures pull her away from her safe place while Caylee tries to fight them off, but her attempts are always in vain.

A while later she was dressed and ready to start her day, one thing she was grateful for was that the Fisher's had an actual bathroom with running water, and although there was no bath or shower, there was a basin for her to at least wash and freshen up.

"Good morning!" Ella chimed when Caylee came down the stairs and entered the kitchen, "Did you sleep well?"

"I did, I almost didn't feel like getting up," she admitted and pulled out a chair to sit down.

Just as she brought the warm steaming cup of tea to her lips the kitchen door opened up and a tall broad shouldered silhouette appeared.

"Caleb!" Ella called out excitedly and ran to pull the man in by his hand, "Where have you been? You were supposed to meet Caylee last night."

Caylee paused with the cup half tilted to her mouth and her heart skipped a beat. Caleb, who Ella often spoke about, stood looking down at her with this broody intimidating look on his face. Unlike Ella he had dark brown hair and striking blue eyes that could probably look right into her sinful soul. She placed her cup down and stood up, extending her hand.

"Hi Caleb, it's a pleasure to meet you," she said.

Caleb looked down at her hand and then simply nodded; barely sparing her a smile, then muttered something to his sister in Dutch and walked into the house.

Ella shrugged and sat down opposite Caylee, "Don't mind him; he's not very comfortable with strangers."

"That's quite alright," Caylee smiled and took her cup again, "I suppose I'm a stranger to him, and I really came here to visit you, but what did he say to you just now?"

Ella twisted one of her braids around her finger, "Oh, just that he still doesn't like the fact that we've agreed to have a journalist write about our lives."

"But your parents agreed, right?"

"Of course they did, and so did the bishop. As long as you don't take photos, they don't mind to share what our lives are about to the outsiders."

Caylee laughed, "The outsiders? It sounds like we're aliens from another planet."

"Oh I didn't mean to offend you; it's just that the non-Amish folk guess what we're about. They think coming to Strasburg and enjoying a tour gives them an insight on who we are, but it doesn't."

Caylee lowered her eyes and frowned, she could just not get over the fact that Amish people are a tourist attraction like Zoo animals, when all they really are, are people with a belief that's grounded in history. But she was really no different, she had come under the false pretenses of sharing the truth about the Amish culture on her news blog, when she was really after the secrets behind Gonder Mansion. She knew she should have told Ella the truth, but she simply convinced herself that the ghost stories were as much a part of the small town as the very culture.

"Doesn't it every upset you that the outsiders consider you to be some tourist attraction on display for their amusement?"

Ella tilted her head and looked at Caylee, "Sometimes, but you have to understand where they come from. Caleb hates it, but I don't really mind. Jesus also attracted crowds of people, just because he was different."

Ella had a point there, she realized and put down her cup, "Good point, so what's on the agenda today?" she asked changing the subject.

"Well I have to go to school and teach, so Caleb will be showing you around."

"Caleb?" Caylee asked surprised.

Ella nodded, "Ya, Daed said he must show you around, it will be fine, I promise."

Somehow Caylee didn't believe her friend. Her first contact with Caleb was cold; he didn't seem to like her at all, but beggars can't be choosers and if she was going to have to settle for Caleb, then so be it.

Chapter 3

Caleb rummaged through his trunk in his room, not looking for anything in particular, but simply trying to keep his hands busy. He was still upset that his father was insisting that he took the reporter around town to show her their culture, he could think of a lot of other things to do. But what unnerved him even more is that she was so beautiful. Her long red hair that fell in waves around her shoulders should be tucked under a bonnet, and she really should be wearing something a lot more modest than the floral printed dress she had on. For starters all the eligible young men in Strasburg would be tempted by the likes of her. It was as if the devil himself sent her into their midst. She was like a Delilah waiting to trap Samson.

When he finally managed to tame his irritation, he went back to the kitchen where, as expected, *Delilah* sat with her computer.

"That's not allowed in the house," he muttered.

"Oh, uh, your dad said it was okay," she challenged as she looked at him.

"Not while I'm around. You need to change your clothes too," he simply said and walked over to the fridge, "I'm not going around town with you looking like you're doing some sort of fashion parade."

She objected and crossed her arms, "What's wrong with my dress?"

He gave her one stern look and bit into an apple and she instantly backed down.

"I-I don't have anything else to wear."

"Ella has, I'm sure she won't mind," he mumbled and then walked out of the kitchen to wait for her outside.

For a split second he felt bad for being so abrupt, but he couldn't have this *Delilah* tag along with him and tempt every young man in town.

When she joined him a few minutes later, he's eyes grew wide, she deliberately ignored his instruction. Instead of putting on a modest Amish dress, she simply put on a shawl to cover her shoulders.

"Why didn't you get one of Ella's dresses," he scolded.

Caylee walked up to him and shoved her finger against his chest, "First of all, I take no instruction from you, and secondly, I think my dress is pretty modest in comparison to what I could wear, so live with it."

Caleb stood gob smacked as she shoved past him and walked to the small wooden gate. This girl, no this woman was going to be the end of him yet. Without a further word, he followed her out the gate and then marched down the street. He could feel the eyes of his friends following them and he wanted to be swallowed whole. He could already hear their taunts about the girl.

"Caleb wait!" she called as he walked ahead.

"Keep up with me, or go on your own expedition," he called over his shoulder.

"Do you have to be such a dweeb?" she called out.

He stopped in his tracks and slowly turned to look at her. Her willow green eyes were hard and cold as she glared at him, but the way her lips pouted was far too tempting. And instead of retaliating he turned around and walked ahead, frustrated as ever.

Chapter 4

Caylee had to give it to Caleb, he was a stubborn as any man, but she was not going to let him intimidate her. He either accepted her for who she was or he could refuse to show her around. But once they got over their initial tiff, things were slightly better. He spoke when he needed to, and she kept conversation to a minimum, in the end it was a rather pleasant morning. Caleb took her around to show her the dairy farm; she got to taste unpasteurized milk and goats' cheese. He took her to meet Bishop Alder, who happened to be a very staunch but pleasant old man. As for the rest of the locals, they all seemed to be pretty normal towards her. She assumed with the amount of tourists that flooded Strasburg at times, they were used to having strangers curiously milling around.

"So, when I was on my way here Sam told me about the ghosts, is it true?" she asked him as they walked back towards the house.

Caleb chuckled, "If you believe in ghosts I suppose they are real."

"Do you believe in them?"

He shook his head, "No I don't, and I really don't think you should be snooping around looking for ghost tales."

Moment over, Caleb was back to his old self, "If you don't believe in ghosts, why worry if I go and snoop? I want to see the Gonder Mansion."

"Not happening," he muttered and stalked ahead.

Cayley hurried after him, "Well then I'll just ask Ella to take me."

Caleb stopped, and she almost crashed into him.

"Listen, you're here to write about the Amish, not dig up old wives tales of dead people who supposedly haunt the town. If you're looking for authentic, stick to what you see around you."

She glared at him and sucked in a breath. Maybe he wasn't the best person to take her site seeing and if she had to be honest, it was almost as if he was hiding something from her.

By the time they reached the house, Ella was already waiting for her, and without as much as a wave, Caleb went on his way. She couldn't help but smile to herself, realizing that Caleb was more bark than bite.

"Did you enjoy the morning?" Ella asked as they made their way into the house.

"It was pleasant," she smiled.

"I know Caleb can be very stubborn, but he's really a nice man," Ella said softly.

"I'm yet to see his nice side."

Ella laughed, "And you will, just give it a few days."

I highly doubt that, she thought following Ella into the house. If she had to spend another morning in Caleb's company she would undoubtedly go insane. She didn't care if he was the most handsome Amish man she had ever laid eyes on, if he didn't have the... *wait what, handsome?* Caylee shook her head to clear the mental image of Caleb lifting the heavy wooden beam of the stable door causing the muscles under his shirt to flex. She couldn't possibly have found that attractive! But here she was thinking about him and the way his blond hair fell over his eyes from under his hat and the way dimples set in his cheeks when he occasionally smiled or chuckled, not to mention that timber voice that tugged at her heart strings.

"Tea?" Ella's voice broke into Caylee's thoughts.

"What?"

Ella tilted her head slightly, "Would you like some tea?"

"Oh, no thanks, I'm fine," she smiled awkwardly.

"Well then, can I show you my Daed's library? He's very fond of books."

Anything that could distract her would help right now, "That would be lovely, what sort of books does he have?"

"Oh just about everything permitted, bibles from most era's, some religious Amish books," she grinned and nudged Caylee with her shoulder, "He even has some of the contemporary Amish romance books."

Surprised Caylee raised her brows, "Your dad reads romance books?"

"Oh heavens no, he just collects them, but my Mamm reads sometimes," Ella giggled.

Caylee was stumped by the amount of books Mr Fisher had in his library, as small as it was, the walls were lined with shelves full of books, but not being one for romance novels, she went straight for the older books. Some still bound with leather and engraved by hand on the spines. She had always been a fan of books especially those with such character. Just trying to comprehend how many hands those books had passed through and how each book was interpreted by the reader at any given time was an intriguing mystery.

"These are absolutely beautiful; do you know what libraries would give to have these books in their archives?" Caylee commented as she ran her fingers along the spines of the books.

"Oh we've had people offering to purchase some, but my daed would never get rid of them, these books have been in our family for decades," Ella commented as she walked over to a glass showcase in the corner of the dim lit room, "This is one of the oldest family bibles in our community," she said and carefully lifted the overly large book from the shelf and placed it on the large oak desk.

Bound in brown leather and cracked and dry from aging, the thick heavy book smelled oddly like stale tobacco. The pages were the color of used tea bags and brittle, and the stitching of the book had withered with age.

As Caylee opened up the great book, she found a faint scrawl on the inside of the cover, which was written in Dutch and the opposite page contained a list of names, which looked like a family tree. So caught up in the moment, she hardly paid attention when Ella's mother called her to help her with the laundry, that Caylee hadn't noticed her friend was gone, but when she did, she took out her phone and snapped a few pictures of the book itself and the first two pages. The rule was that she was not allowed to take photos of the people, but no one said she wasn't allowed to take a photo of an old book.

Glancing around her she looked for a place with more light to lean the book against so that she could capture its authenticity as much as she could. A small table right next to the window was the perfect spot. She carefully picked the bible up and carried it over to the table, but as she stood it on its side, a folded piece of paper floated almost weightlessly to the floor.

"What have we here," she chimed to herself as she picked the supposed letter up off the floor. It had the same withered look as the bible which means this letter was probably decades old. She cautiously unfolded the piece of paper, careful not to ruin it since the folds in the letter had already settled deep into the thin paper and any disturbance could tear it.

Much to her surprise it wasn't a letter, but rather a map which she found rather odd. What would a map possibly do in a bible unless it was used as a book mark? But her gut told her otherwise. It was hand drawn and the odd word she could make out on the points of interest seemed like it was a map of Strasburg. A diagonal line ran from what looked like a church or cemetery to a spot with the letter A.G. At first it didn't make much sense, but then she recalled the story of Annie, the girl who haunts Strasburg and specifically Gonder Mansion. Could this be a map be related to the hauntings? Intrigued by what she found she sat down and studied the map further.

"Do you always make a habit of snooping around?"

Caleb. Her heart skipped a beat, "I'm not snooping, and Ella was showing me the family bible."

Caleb looked down at the map in front of her, and a frown settled between his brows, "Where did you get that?" he snapped and reached for it, but Caylee blocked his attempts with her hand.

"It fell out of the bible," she breathed.

"This was supposed to have been destroyed," he muttered and went to close the door.

Shocked at his words, Caylee picked the map up and folded it closed, "What do you mean destroyed?"

"He remembers our sins and lawlessness no more," he murmured and held out his hand, "Give it to me."

"Who remembers what?" Caylee asked and took a step back, "What are you talking about?"

"The past is in the past, that map should have been destroyed a long time ago."

Caylee had enough, she wasn't going to let Caleb take away her bit of mystery, she needed to know what this was, and what its purpose was.

"I tell you what, you take me to Gonder Mansion tomorrow, and I'll give it back to you once I've seen the ghost for myself," she whispered.

Caleb regarded her, his brows drawn together and his face pale, but instead of arguing, he nodded, "We'll go on Friday night, when everyone is asleep."

She extended her hand and grinned, "Deal, then you can have the map."

Chapter 5

The next few days Caylee spent most of her time site seeing and tagging along with Ella to get to know the community. She joined in on a quilting sessions where she learned how to quilt. She had hoped to go to one of the barn raisings the Amish was so well known for, but that was not on the cards. Other than that, she did daily chores like every other Amish woman, from peeling potatoes to washing clothes on a laundry board. But even as simple as they were, she never missed city life. This existence, the peace and tranquility was something she could grow accustomed to. More and more she found herself wondering what life would be like if she ever converted to become Amish.

It was one afternoon when she went with Ella to collect eggs from the coops when she noticed Caleb working in one of the fields. As they passed, she could sense his eyes resting on her but she refused to look in his directly. Seemingly indifferent she jabbered on about how she hated the city.

"I think Caleb likes you," Ella said out of the blue.

Caylee laughed and looked at her friend, "Are you stark raving mad? What on earth gives you such an idea?"

Ella shrugged, "He's my brother, and I've seen him look at girls, but he's never looked at them the same way he looks at you."

"That's silly, he hates me."

Ella slapped her shoulder playfully, "Hate is not part of our faith, but I can see the way he looks at you. Haven't you noticed?"

That made her glance in his direction and as true as there was a sun in the sky, Caleb was leaning on a rake looking straight at them. She awkwardly raised her hand and wiggled her fingers before casting her eyes to the ground, "He's not used to city girls, that's all."

"If you say so," giggled Ella and skipped off, "Last one at the coop is a rotten egg!"

Friday night had arrived, and like every other night they all had dinner, and afterward Caylee helped Ella do the dishes, while Caleb and his dad caught up on business. When she had finally made it to bed, she was exhausted, but that could not stifle her excitement. She kept checking her phone to make sure she had enough battery life, and then she walked to the window to see if there was any sign of Caleb. She was both excited and nervous she waited impatiently for him to come and get her.

She had been on the verge of going to find him when she heard a small tick on the window. Outside in the dark she could hardly see anything, other than the silhouettes of trees lining the sky in front of the waning moon. She opened the window and stuck her head out.

"Caleb?" she whispered.

"I'm here," he said in a hushed tone from under her window, "I'll help you down."

Her heart was beating a million miles a second, this was wrong in so many ways. She felt like she was back in high school, sneaking off with Marc to go to parties while her parents were fast asleep in bed. She worried her lip and looked to her left if she could reach the trellis next to her window she could use that as a ladder to get down.

"Give me a sec," she said and ducked back into the room. Wearing a dress was no option, so instead she quickly changed into a pair of jeans and a thick sweater before she headed back to the window. "Will this hold me?"

"Yes, come we don't have all night."

Caylee stuck one leg through the window and reached for the trellis, then pulled herself on to the structure that was mounted firmly against the wall. Too scared to take a breath, she slowly climbed her way down, careful not to miss a step. She was a few feet from the ground when she heard a loud CRACK! And then her support was gone, and she felt herself free-falling.

Caleb was fast, and before she could hit the ground, he caught her effortlessly. How she managed to hold back a squeal was another story, but as she looked up at him, she was sure she saw a smile tug at the corners of his mouth.

"You don't do this often do you?" he said amusedly.

"Did you suddenly discover you have a sense of humor?" she bit back jokingly.

"There's a lot about me that you would never know."

Pointe made, sense of humor lost. Caylee rolled her eyes and scrambled out of his arms, but even as she stood away from him she could still feel the heat of his body against hers. *Madness, utter madness,* she thought and shrugged, "So? Are we going to Gonder Mansion?"

"Follow me," he whispered.

Caleb was frustrated, all his life here in Strasburg, he'd been nothing but an obedient son, and a well-mannered young man, but since Caylee arrived in town, he's been on edge. Not only was she a beautiful young woman, she was a soulful woman and one who did not take no for an answer. He liked that about her. He liked the fact that she was so different to Amish girls who tend to submit rather than stand their ground. If there was ever one thing he'd change about the Amish ways, it would be to have women become more than just cooks and nannies.

As they made their way through the field towards the Gonder Mansion, he was fully aware of her at all times. The way her breath rushed out of her lungs in huffs when he walked to fast, or the way she sniffed against the cold hair. Every single sound she made was like a melody to him.

"So what made you decide to do a story about the Amish?" he asked, attempting for small talk.

She shrugged, "Curiosity I guess. I mean, why Amish people would subject themselves to be tourist attractions like animals in a zoo makes no sense. I find it demeaning and I think it's time someone shows the world that Amish are just normal people." It was a blatant lie. She was here for one thing and one thing only, to find the Ghost of Gonder mansion.

"Are we really normal? I mean, we don't rely on electricity, we have no motorcars, and some of the older families do not even have running water in their houses. We live as if we were in the middle ages."

"So? That doesn't mean anything. It's your human right to live as you please."

Amused by her firm opinion he smiled, "I guess you're not all that bad then."

"I suppose you judged me before you even got to know me," she countered.

"That is true," he said and shrugged, "but in my defense, we've had journalists here before and all they ever do is judge."

"So you generalized."

Caleb chuckled, and stopped, "The Gonder mansion is up ahead, are you sure you want to go there?"

Caylee pulled out the map and took out her cell phone to use its flashlight, "I'm intrigued to see where the map leads," she said distractedly.

"Here," he said and pulled out another piece of paper, "You'll need this part to complete the puzzle."

Caleb opened up his piece of paper and laid it on top of the one Caylee had, and the look of confusion on her face was no surprise. When he stumbled on her in his dad's library, he didn't expect to find her there, with the map he'd been looking for since he was about thirteen years old.

According to most, Mr Gonder kept his daughter Annie locked away in the house to keep her from scaring the people of Strasburg. She was thought to be mentally ill, and after her reported drowning in the nearby Pequea Creek, the stories of her haunting the mansion and the cemetery surfaced. Back in the day, ghosts were considered evil spirits and people feared the unknown. He had heard the story when he was just a boy, and had since been so captivated by it, that he did extensive research on the history of Gonder Mansion. It wasn't until he found his map that he realized the haunted stories were simply ways to keep unwanted treasure seekers away from the Gonder fortunes. Not that he was a fortune seeker, but if this was indeed a treasure of sorts, he could prove to the entire world that they were fooled by ghost stories.

"Where did you get this?" Caylee asked in awe as she moved her phone under the two pieces of paper.

"I've had it for some time," he simply said and then lined the two pages up.

With the traced lines from his map, shining through on the top map, he could clearly see where X marks the spot, it wasn't at the Gonder mansion after all; the treasure was in fact, in the cemetery.

"What exactly am I looking at?" Caylee asked curiously.

"This dear lady is a treasure map to the Gonder fortunes, or so I believe. You see, the ghost story of Annie was simply Mr Gonder's way to hide the truth and prevent his greedy family to lay rightful claim to his property, or well, in this case his fortunes."

"But why would you be looking for treasures, isn't that some sort of sin?"

"Only if I want it for personal gain, right now I just want to prove to the world that ghosts do not exist."

Caylee looked at him and frowned, "How long have you known about this?"

"Since I was about sixteen when I found this map, the elders of the town always denied it, but I just had this feeling that there was more to this ghost story than meets the eye."

Caylee followed Caleb down the footpath that led through the small forest towards the cemetery. She hated cemetery's, it reminded her of the many souls that lay there awaiting their final judgement, or worse, those souls who have unfinished business and who made it their mission to scare the living daylights out of people they despise.

"This way," Caleb said and reached for her hand, "We'll go through the west gate, it's always unattended."

When Caylee placed her hand in his, Caleb's heart skipped a beat and he cleared his throat. Her hands were soft and warm, unlike the hands of the hard working Amish women who work and toil all day.

"Do you come here often?" she whispered.

He chuckled, "No I don't, but I know the ground keeper."

They made their way round the side wall towards the west gate, and all the way there, Caylee felt as if a million eyes were on her and amongst them her secret.

"You're nervous, do you believe in ghosts?" Caleb asked when they reached the gate.

She glanced past him, over his shoulder towards the towering tombstones that looked like crooked teeth sticking out of the ground, "Will you judge me if I do?"

"Ghosts are aspirations of past transgressions, it's a person's mind playing tricks on them because they have unresolved issues there simply are no ghosts."

Caylee swallowed, if ever a nail was hit into a coffin with precision, this would have been it. Were the ghosts she felt staring at her, her own secrets that haunted her? Was she so vulnerable that she was projecting her own fears on to an unseen entity?

"Do other Amish believe in ghosts?"

Caleb shook his head and moved ahead into the cemetery without saying a word and Caylee followed close by. Believing in the unseen was silly, but the way she felt now, she was sure there were many souls carefully watching them.

Chapter 6

They made their way through the cemetery, following the map until they reached a large tree that stood in the middle and for a moment she thought about the garden of Eden and she was Eve about to bit into the forbidden fruit.

"Are you sure it's safe here?" she asked as a shiver ran through her.

"Ya, it's perfectly safe," Caleb reassured her.

Around the tree was a wrought iron fence, and on the stump of the tree was a wooden plaque with the words, *A. M. Gonder, Beloved Daughter 1896—1918.* This must have been Annie's burial ground, she realized as she followed Caleb into the small enclosure.

"If this map is what I think it is, there should be something behind this plaque," Caleb said and felt around the sides.

"This doesn't feel right," Caylee objected hugging her arms around her waist.

"A journalist with a conscience, that's new," he smirked, "I thought you'd kill for a story like this."

Caylee huffed and rolled her eyes, "I'm a journalist not a tomb raider," she muttered.

"We're not unearthing her body, so relax."

Easy for you to say, she thought as she glanced around her.

Caleb took a pocket knife from his pocket and flicked open the blade then wedged it in between the plaque and the tree. He groaned and twisted the blade until the plaque tore away. She raised her phone and shone the light on the opening behind the plaque, but instead of finding treasure there was a small wooden box, and inside it a letter. Caleb took the letter out and opened it up while Caylee used the light from her phone.

"What does it say?" she asked curiously, unable to read Dutch.

Caleb lowered himself to the ground, and she joined him, studying his face.

"It's an apology letter," he murmured, "It looks like it's from her mother."

"Okay, but what does it say?" she asked again.

"So apparently, Annie's mother had fallen in love with another man, and that was how she was conceived. Her husband, Mr Gonder was so enraged that he used to beat her when she was with child..."

Caylee's heart cramped, what a terrible thing to experience, she thought.

Caleb continued, "When Annie was born, she had already been a victim of the abuse and had mental challenges. Her mother says that she never meant for anyone to get hurt, and she begged her daughter for forgiveness."

Caleb grew silent and frowned.

"What is it?" Caylee asked and scooted closer to him.

"*I had no choice my dear daughter, you have suffered enough. I should have sent you home to heaven when you were still in my womb, but I always hoped that things would get better. Your brother and father have learned the truth, they know you are with child, and before they can harm you or your baby, I have no choice but to lay you to rest myself. I'm so sorry. God help me.*"

The last words echoed in her head as Caleb translated the last part of the letter word for word and tears filled her eyes. Annie's mother wanted to abort her daughter when she was still pregnant, and she could never go through with it. And then years later, she drowned her mentally ill daughter herself. What a terrible, terrible thing to do.

Caylee sucked in a shaky breath and stood up, which was the lesser of two evils? She wondered as she headed blindly in the direction they came from.

"Caylee! Wait!" Caleb called, but she simply walked on.

She couldn't stand it, she couldn't even comprehend what poor Annie had to go through, and how much she was hated by those who were supposed to protect her. But it wasn't only Annie's story that upset her, it was her own.

She had been out partying with her friends when she landed herself in quite a predicament. One of their friends had one too many to drink and when things got out of hand he had forced himself on her. She only had herself to blame, she kept telling herself, but when she discovered she was pregnant she couldn't go through with it. And against her moral values, she had the baby aborted. It was one of the hardest choices she ever had to make, and a choice she had come to regret.

"Caylee, what's the matter," Caleb asked as he fell into step next to her.

"Nothing," she muttered under her breath.

"Well something upset you; do you want to talk about it?"

She shook her head, refusing to let him see her tears and simply stumbled ahead in the darkness. Caleb's tone of voice was almost endearing and that hurt even more. She didn't deserve anything; she sure as hell did not deserve to be alive.

"Caylee, running won't make you feel better," he said and pulled her to a stop.

"What do you know about feeling better or running? You're stuck in this cocooned life milking cows for a living, you don't have the foggiest about life and what goes on out there!" she spat out and tugged her arm free.

He didn't even flinch, although she was almost sure that her words hurt him, "How could that woman kill her own daughter and her unborn grandchild?" she said in a trembling voice.

Caleb frowned, "You're upset about something that happened almost a century ago?"

"No! Yes, I mean, if she didn't want her daughter in the first place, why wait until Annie was old enough to have her own children before she so heartlessly drowned her in the creek?"

This time Caleb reacted and as he pulled her into his arms and held her against his chest, she couldn't hold back the tears any longer. She had never known affection, even as a child, growing up, her parents were never the kiss and cuddle type. Her dad had been too busy working night and day to make ends meet while her mother spent most of the time sulking about her loveless marriage. Her relationships always turned out a disaster simply because she had no idea how to show her feelings, and now here with Caleb, it felt as if a switch has been flipped. She hardly knew him, but he made her feel safe and secure.

"It will all be alright," he whispered against her hair, "Wherever Annie is, I'm sure she's in a much better place."

Caylee smiled through her tears against his chest. Here he was thinking she was crying over Annie, when this whole thing was about her, and what she had done, but even though he had no idea what was going on in her mind and heart, she consoled herself with the fact that he cared.

Chapter 7

A week had passed since the discovery of the letter in the cemetery and not surprisingly, Caleb had been avoiding her ever so slightly. He was Amish; their dating customs are different to the outside world. She was a modern woman with a life waiting for her in the city, there could never be anything between her and Caleb and for all that she knew, her feelings were unrequited, she was not his type.

It was just past four in the morning, and she couldn't sleep, so instead she pulled out her laptop. It was about time she started to pen down something about the Amish of Strasburg. At some point in time Ella was going to ask her to see what she wrote, and she simply could not disappoint her friend. She stared at the screen for a while and its blank white soul stared back at her with the cursor flickering at the top left corner of the page. Where would she start?

The ghost of Strasburg... a story told through the ages was nothing but a memory of a girl who lived, loved and died. The fact of the matter is that there are no ghosts, only the ghosts of your own past, which come to haunt and taunt us. Memories we try to ignore as if they were nothing but a figment of our imagination, manifesting into goblins and ghouls that make things go bump at night and deprives us of our sanity. Well this is my story, and this is my ghost...

The words flowed effortlessly; it had been months since she was able to put anything to paper. Her inspiration was drained and writers block had set in, but it was finally over. She had moved out of limbo and she was about to write the biggest most brilliant piece yet.

She was at least halfway with her article when there was a slight knock on the door and her heart instantly skipped a beat and the first person that came to mind was Caleb. But she knew Caleb would never knock on her door.

"Come in," she called and pushed her chair away from the desk.

"Will you be joining us for church?" Ella asked as she peeked into the room.

She had skipped church since she got here, but this morning was another story, something deep down urged her to get up.

"Sure," she said and Ella's face lit up.

"You can borrow one of my dresses," her friend said excitedly and dashed back to her room.

A little while later, Ella returned with a purple dress, a white apron and cape and

"I can help you dress," Ella said and hung the dress on a hook behind the door.

Caylee smiled. This was going to be a first for her. She looked at the dress and then at Ella, she knew her friend was eager to help, and although dressing was second nature, she nodded, "That would be nice."

An hour later, the two girls took a leisurely stroll down the road to the church. It was a small white building constructed of wood and surrounded with neatly trimmed trees and grass and red doors as the entrance. Caylee paused and took a deep steadying breath. She had no idea how the rest of the people would react to seeing her wearing traditional Amish clothes when she wasn't even close to being Amish, but if Ella didn't see any problem with it, then why should they?

"Caleb!" Ella called and waved her hand above her hear.

Caylee's heart drummed against her chest and she slowly turned around. When Caleb laid eyes on her, he stopped in his tracks. His eyes wide with surprise at first and then a slow smile crept across his lips.

"Oh he likes you alright," Ella whispered with unmoving lips as she leaned closer to her.

"Oh shush you," she huffed and felt a blush wash over her face.

Caleb walked over to the two of them and when he reached them he grinned, "I see you found some suitable clothes to wear to church today."

She cleared her throat and gave a sideways pout, "Ella insisted."

"Did she now?" he said with a raised brow.

"Yes she did. If I had my way, I wouldn't…"

Caleb held up his hand and smiled, "You look beautiful."

That had her swallow her words, the way he said it was almost like a fleeting breeze on a hot summers day, she mumbled a barely audible thank you and then spun around and followed Ella into the church. But she could feel Caleb's gaze on her back.

The service was much like any other church service she had been to, with the exception that there were no musical instruments, and the unmarried women and men sat on opposite sides of the isle. Two rows from the back, Caylee sat right up against the isle and whether it was deliberate or not, Caleb sat across from her on the other side of the isle. They might as well have been sitting right next to each other.

Throughout the service she tried to focus on the sermon but every now and again she glanced sideways only to find him looking at her. She was starting to slowly like the attention from him, but she couldn't possibly fit into his world. She forced her attention back to the sermon and kept her attention on the bishop. He was talking about forgiveness, not only about forgiving others but also forgiving one's own transgressions. The things done to oneself, in secret, hatred, regret, guilt, all of these things prevent a person from growing spiritually and being free in Christ Jesus.

As the words of the sermon sunk in she felt a stirring in her soul, she had so many demons that kept her from being who she was meant to be, and living like this, in fear and condemnation was debilitating, but how could she forgive herself for what she had done?

"Blessed is he whose transgressions are forgiven, whose sins are covered. Blessed is the man whose sin the LORD does not count against him and in whose spirit is no deceit. When I kept silent, my bones wasted away through my groaning all day long. For day and night your hand was heavy upon me; my strength was sapped as in the heat of summer. Then I acknowledged my sin to you and did not cover up my iniquity. I said, 'I

will confess my transgressions to the LORD'—and you forgave the guilt of my sin."

Caylee raised her head and looked at the bishop and her eyes shot full of tear, could it even be so easy? She wondered. A simple prayer to God to forgive her sins, would be all it took. The rest of the sermon was a blur, all she could think about was the abortion, and Annie, the poor girl who didn't deserve to die such a cruel death.

After the sermon, she opted to go home instead of joining the lunch festivities with the rest, she needed time to herself, time to reflect on her past and how she was going to get over what she had done all those months ago.

She was sitting in the kitchen sipping a glass of lemonade when she heard the front door open and close. Expecting to see Ella entering the kitchen she was quite surprised to find Caleb standing in the doorway.

"Are you alright?" he asked with his hands tucked in his pockets.

"Yeah, I'm fine," she whispered, fighting back the tears.

Caleb stepped forward and took out a piece of cloth, laying it down in front of her, "I found this, maybe it will make you feel better?"

She looked down at the brown tattered fabric, there was something inside it and she carefully opened it up. A silver rattle with the words—*To my angel Annie*—engraved on it.

She looked up at Caleb and frown drew her brows together, "Where did you find this?"

He pulled a chair closer and took the rattle from her, "I found it in the tree, behind the letter. Her mother loved her, but she couldn't protect her, even as a little baby."

"But she killed her," Caylee whispered.

"Out of love, she did, but you see. Annabelle Gonder was my mother's great grandmother, which is why I was so adamant to prove that ghosts do not exist. This whole thing had been a burden on our family and although many had forgotten about it over the years, some of the older people still found it hard to believe what really happened.

I needed to find out the truth for myself, and for my Mamm so that she too could seek absolution for the sins her great grandmother committed. But I couldn't have done it without you, don't you see? You coming here to Strasburg was God's plan," he smiled and gently laid his hand on hers.

She looked down at their hands and closed her eyes, "Caleb, there's something I need to tell you," she started and swallowed nervously.

"You can tell me anything," he said and cupped his other hand over hers.

"I was upset about Annie, and how she died, but..." she paused and took a shaky breath, "I'm not much different to her mother..."

Once she started she couldn't stop, she told Caleb about the incident at the club, and how she ended up pregnant and then how she decided to have an abortion. Throughout Caleb never judged her, he listened, he really listened. And for the first time since that horrible day, she didn't feel alone.

"... So you see, I'm not without sin, I've done terrible things."

Caleb smiled and scooted his chair closer, wrapping one arm around her shoulders, "But you are forgiven, and that's all that matters. Your sins were your own, but now they are God's and if you let me, I can walk this road with you."

Caylee's heart bounced wildly in her chest as she leaned into Caleb's embrace. Maybe this was the grand design after all. Nothing happens without a reason, and sometimes the road to healing is a hard and cruel road full of obstacles, but in the end the reward is invaluable.

She tilted his head and glanced up at him, "I would like that," she whispered and leaned her head against his shoulder.

~*~

Caylee sat on the quilt in the open field where Caleb paced up and down with their baby girl Annie in his arms. Her life changed forever, and forgiveness now her strength, she smiled and looked down at the small poem she wrote to her lost child.

So fragile

so small

tiny hands

perfect fingers

and tippy toes

thrown into a world

where lies freely fall

If I could have kept you

I would

safe from rage

broken lies

inevitable pain

Safe in my arms

Wrapped in my heart

Forever

I love you always... my sweet little Alissa

1 Jon 1:9

If we confess our sins, he is faithful and just to forgive us our sins and to cleanse us from all unrighteousness.

AMISH SUNDAY

ELAINE LANE

A yellow taxi sped down the PA 340, also known as the Old Philadelphia Pike. The driver threw curious glances at his passenger through the rearview mirror. She had given him directions to take the backroads towards the Amish town of Bird-in-hand, but she wasn't dressed "plain" like most of the locals there. Her thick auburn hair was uncovered—no bonnet or cap like he'd seen Amish girls wear—though gathered in a neat coil at the base of her neck. But something about the simplicity of her white blouse, the long blue skirt, and the fraying wool cardigan she wore made him think that she wasn't a tourist, or someone who belonged in the city. Maybe it was her lack of interest in the sprawling, golden farmlands they had passed on the way here that gave her the air of a local.

At the last town they had driven through, the Conestoga river had been a sight to behold; a long trail of blue water, extending past the horizon on either side of the bridge. It had sparkled brightly under the sun, as pretty as anything. But his passenger hadn't even blinked an eye and she hadn't spoken more than a sentence since she had gotten in the car about half an hour ago. Her eyes were puffy then, like she had been crying recently, so he'd shut his trap and kept his curiosity to himself. But some small talk now wouldn't hurt, right?

"Are you here for a visit, Miss?" Through the rearview mirror, he could see her look up from her reading—a pocket Bible he guessed.

"I left near the end of my *rumspringa,*" she said. He glanced at the mirror again and caught a sad smile on her face. The look in the young woman's eyes was old and tired. The poor girl couldn't be more than nineteen or twenty. "But I'm back now."

"Ah, *rumspringa,*" the old driver said. "The time of youth 'running around.' So you've made your choice then?"

"Even though I'm a few years late," she said, fiddling around in the back seat. It sounded like she was stowing away her Bible. She snapped her weather-beaten carpet bag shut. "I've come back to be baptized. If the Lord will take me back."

"What are you talking about?" he said, watching the road. In the distance, he could just see the outline of a horse and buggy in the shoulder lane, approaching at an ambling walk. And far to the right, a sign post with an arrow that said, "Exit—Smoketown." After driving past Smoketown, they'd arrive at Bird-in-hand. "Of course the Lord will want you back," he said. "I may not be Amish, but I know that much about Him."

She was quiet for awhile. "Bless you for your kind words," she said. "But. . ." She trailed off and was quiet for so long that the old driver figured it was the end of their talk. Then suddenly, she said, "Could you drop me off here?"

"What?" he said, sitting up in surprise. "Here? Now? At the side of the road?"

"Yes, please," she said. "If you don't mind."

"Was it something I said?"

"No. I didn't mean to make you think that," she said. "But the prodigal daughter returning home in a motorized car?" She shakes her head. "We're in Smoketown now. I can walk from here."

##

Esther Miller shaded her eyes, squinting through the glare of the sun on the pavement, as she watched the yellow taxi turn into a dot in the horizon, heading back to Lancaster City. When she couldn't see it anymore, she turned around, picked up her bags and started walking. The gravel at the side of the road was difficult to walk on, the loose stones kept shifting under her shoes. Gusts of wind kicked up swirls of dust into her face so she walked with her eyes nearly half shut.

She ducked her head down and brought her arm up against another onslaught of dirt and leaves, but this time the wind carried with it something else: the sound of an infant's cries. When the gust died down, she straightened and spotted a horse and buggy standing by on the opposite side of the road. She couldn't see a driver, but the crying seemed to come from that direction. She gripped her carpet bag and crossed the empty highway.

Later on she would wonder what had really driven her to follow the sound—if it was curiosity, a desire to be of help, or if it was her own fresh grief. The closer she got to the buggy, the louder the the baby's cries grew. It wasn't just that she was getting nearer to the baby, it sounded like. . . it sounded like the baby was wailing out a lament. Those cries sounded to Esther like an echo of her own heart. *O Lord, heal me for my bones are troubled*, she thought. Psalm 6, Verse 2. She came within arms reach of the horse, a brown saddlebred stallion with a splash of white on its forehead, shoulder, and rump. The stallion turned its head to look at her through its blinders and she patted its neck.

It was just as she rounded the buggy, that she heard his voice, mixed in with the baby's cries. He was quietly humming the tune of *Twinkle, Twinkle Little Star* and she caught snatches of Pennsylvanian Dutch words in place of the English lyrics. Esther's heart stopped. She knew that voice. She'd heard that same voice singing that song together with her on quiet, summer evenings by the lake. It was their little inside joke. But where they used to sing it in good fun, now Esther heard only the voice of a tired, helpless man trying to sing something to calm a baby. And failing badly.

She took one more step and there he was: Isaac Beiler. He had grown a short beard, but there was no mistaking that broad back, the slope of those heavy-set shoulders, the disproportionately long legs that she had teased him over because his calves were thinner than hers, and the ginger hair that curled over his nape in ringlets.

"In der Stillen Einsamkeit," he sang, "Findest du mein lob bereit, Grosser Gott—"

"Isaac?" she whispered.

He turned around and looked up at her, his eyes wide. "Essie?" The baby wailed and he rocked it instinctively, his gaze roaming over her face as if he was trying to track all the ways she had changed. She wanted to hide, but she couldn't look away from those brown eyes. "I can't believe it," he said. "Is it really you?"

The baby was almost howling now, red-faced and miserable. Isaac held a feeding bottle to the baby's mouth but the baby turned its head away and kept on crying. Esther noted the blue and white baby clothes. "Your son?" she said.

"Yes," said Isaac. "His name's Aaron. He's going on five months now."

Esther looked at the bottle in Isaac's grip. "His mother isn't here?"

Isaac looked at his son and Esther saw a myriad of things she couldn't read flit over his face. Then he turned to her and she wondered if she had imagined it. There were dark circles under his eyes. "No," he said, without explaining further. "And Aaron won't feed today, no matter what I do. He just keeps crying. I don't know what's wrong."

"May I?" she said, holding out her arms. Isaac blinked at her in surprise, but he passed her the wailing baby without comment. As soon as she held him, Aaron stopped abruptly and stared at Esther in shock, his large blue eyes unblinking.

"What?" Isaac scratched his beard. "How did you?"

Esther cradled the baby close to her breast. "He's distracted trying to figure out who I am and what's going on, right now. He might just resume crying later." The warmth and the weight of the baby in her arms made her breasts ache. She was full again. And the baby's tiny fist had begun to grope instinctively for his mother's breast, the little mouth opening like a hatchling demanding to be fed. Esther's throat closed up and she felt the tears build behind her eyes.

"Isaac," she said. "Isaac, should I . . ."

He stared at her, frozen, as the tears began to drip down her face.

"Should I feed him myself?" Esther said.

He extended the milk bottle to her, wide eyed and awkward in the face of her sudden tears. But Esther was already unbuttoning her white blouse and turning away.

"Wha- what are you doing?" Isaac said, sounding thoroughly confused and a little panicked.

"What does it look like?" she muttered. With her back to him, Esther was grateful that she didn't have to see his face the moment he put two and two together. Baby Aaron took to her breast easily, relaxing, content and pacified in her hold. In the newly formed silence, Esther could hear the horse nickering beside her as it nibbled on the clumps of grass growing by the side of the road. She heard the faint sound of the baby swallowing milk, and feel the little puffs of warm breath on her skin.

When Esther realized that Isaac had been silent too long, minutes had already gone by. She peered behind her cautiously, but he was gone. She cast her gaze around and then further out to the open field beyond the road, but he was nowhere in sight. The baby kept suckling and Esther put away any thoughts of Isaac for the time being.

##

Isaac Beiler crouched next to the buggy's rear wheel, inspecting it again even though he knew it worked perfectly fine. He remembered Esther as a freckle-faced girl, with a laugh as bright as her eyes, and an energy that sparked and burned. She was like a small fire, warm and good, but he had always been aware of a banked potential in her. A potential to turn into something overwhelming. If she was a fire. . . Even as children living next to each other and seeing each other everyday, he had always felt a little bit like a moth, drawn irrevocably to this girl, the dressmaker's third daughter, who was sometimes more boyish and wilder than his own younger brothers. But she always knew when to toe the line. She had been wild but never disobedient or rebellious. She also knew exactly how to circumvent rules without getting into trouble.

Before the two of them entered their *rumspringa,* she used to climb the big oak tree outside the attic room he shared with his two younger brothers, once or twice a week, just before curfew. Often, she'd stay all night, talking and telling stories, sometimes showing off her captive insect of the week, to the delight of his little brothers. Isaac suspected that both of their parents knew, but if they did, they never let on or said anything to condone or condemn Esther's nightly excursions to the neighbor's house.

When the two of them came into their *rumspringa* period, things didn't really change so much as shift into something *more*. Esther climbing into his room at night, to talk like they had always done, became something that either of them—or anyone really—could interpret as 'bundling', except that Isaac's brothers were there too, so it wasn't quite 'bundling'. They never discussed it, but Isaac had felt that she had been waiting.

When Isaac finally managed to purchase his very own courtship buggy and drove it to Sunday evening sing for the first time, she rode with him to church and back without waiting for him to give a formal offer. He had driven her to church of course, because it was just common sense that he would do so. But after the evening sing, that spot next to him on the buggy that was meant for the girl he was courting—it simply became her seat without question.

And so, that first night he drove her home, they had talked and laughed and sang silly songs as they had always done. But something new had begun. Something his teenage self, driving his new girlfriend home on his new buggy for the first time, could have never imagined would end the way it did. . . three years later.

And now, almost five years since that night, Isaac lingered here, crouched by a wheel, trying to occupy himself while Esther suckled his baby son on the other side of the buggy. Footsteps to his right made him look up. Esther stood by the horse's muzzle, baby Aaron in her arms, her English blouse fully buttoned once again.

"I'll be going now," she said, extending Aaron out for Isaac to take. He rose to his feet to accept his now quiet son back, watching as Esther picked up her bag and turned to walk in the direction of Bird-in-hand.

"Esther!" he called out.

She stopped and turned around.

"I'll drive you," said Isaac. "You're going home, aren't you?"

"You're going the other way," she said. Her long blue skirt fluttered around her calves in the wind and wisps of auburn hair blew across her face. She raised a hand to push the stray hair back and for a moment, he thought of walking over and reaching out to tuck those auburn strands behind her ear. The decades old daydream of his teenage self—of untying her kapp, taking out her hairpins one by one, and watching her flame-like hair spill out across her back, loose and free—surfaced again, as vivid as it had always been, embellished by time and... and what?

She turned to go and Isaac realized he had been lost in thought for too long. He deposited the sleeping Aaron in his bassinet, carefully secured into the passenger seat of the buggy, and strapped him in. Esther was still walking. There was no rush because she wasn't going to disappear from the road, but Isaac found himself jumping into the driver's seat and snapping the reins with a little too much haste anyway. He turned the buggy around, back towards Bird-in-hand, and overtook Esther in seconds, the stallion, Pharaoh, cutting across her path.

She stopped and looked up at him, and then away. "I can walk," she said. "We've gone farther on foot before."

"I won't ask," said Isaac. "Whatever it is, I won't ask. But we can still catch up, can't we? We can talk about other things. And Aaron hasn't been this peaceful since... Well, he might cry again." He leaned out from his seat and stole her carpet bag, depositing it in the backseat.

"Hey!" she cried. "Idiot boy!" She scowled at him.

"So it *is* you after all," Isaac said, chuckling. "That's a more familiar look on your face."

Esther's brows shot up and her scowl disappeared.

"Though I'm not a boy anymore," Isaac muttered.

"Your beard's still a bit sparse," she said. Then she sighed and climbed into the passenger seat next to him. Isaac flicked her one last look before he turned his attention back to the road, clicking his tongue and snapping the reins. Pharaoh broke into a trot, and the three of them—Isaac, Esther, and baby Aaron—drove back to Bird-in-hand, back to the open fields of the Beiler Stables and the little property next to it, with the running brook and the white-blooming apple trees: the Millers' home.

"Isaac," she said when they had been driving for a while with nothing but the rhythmic clip clop of hooves to listen to.

"Hmm?" He kept his eyes on the horizon, where the lines on the road seemed to converge.

"Thanks for the ride."

"You're welcome," he said. *I wish you wouldn't thank me*, he thought. If things hadn't gone so wrong all those years ago, when they'd been courting, she wouldn't have to thank him for driving her wherever she needed to go. It would have been his job.

##

A quarter of a mile from the Miller's place, they came across two young women in blue dresses and matching white aprons and kapps, with baskets on their hips, walking by the side of the dirt road at the edge of the Stoltzfus' field. They waved a greeting to Isaac when they caught sight of him.

"Are you back so soon, Mr. Beiler?" one of them called out. "Weren't you taking your son to a doctor in the city?" The woman who spoke was tall and slender, with bright blue eyes and golden curls under her kapp. Esther marveled that she could seem so beautiful despite her plain dress.

"Well," Isaac rubbed at the back of his neck, "it seems like little Aaron might not need a doctor after all."

"Oh, that's good news," the woman said with a graceful, bubbling laugh. "The Lord heard your prayers, didn't He?"

"Ah, yes," Isaac said, looking mildly embarrassed.

And then the woman's eyes landed on Esther and she paused, uncertain. Her companion peered curiously at Esther as well.

Esther had known most of the young folk who were around her age, especially the ones in her singing group. But she didn't know everyone, and these girls might have been too young for her to be familiar with. "I'm Esther Miller," she said. "Dressmaker Miller's daughter."

"Oh," the woman said. "The Miller's? Then the two of you are old neighbors? I've heard so much about you from the Beiler boys. Please call me Judith. And this is Beth."

Beth smiled and waved just as Isaac cleared his throat beside Esther.

"You ladies must have errands to run," he said. "We shouldn't be keeping you from it. Good day." Isaac flicked the reins and they drove off, leaving both the girls and Esther puzzled.

"That was rude of you," said Esther.

Isaac flushed and shrugged. "It was, but. . ."

"But?"

"It's complicated," he said. "Judith and I. . . It's too early for me to think about things like that when not even a year ago. . . just five months ago. . ."

Esther knew now that she had guessed right. "Aaron was born and then your wife. . ?

"There were complications," said Isaac. "The midwife did everything she could but. . ."

"What was her name? Did I know her?"

"Rosemarie," he said.

Oh, thought Esther, *of course he married Rosemarie*. Rosemarie had been the kindest, prettiest girl in their youth group. Esther had sometimes felt clumsy and self-centered next to Rosemarie, but she couldn't help but like the girl. Everyone liked Rosemarie. Esther reached a hand into the bassinet sandwiched between her and the driver's seat, and stroked baby Aaron's soft cheek, flushed with health. *So you are Rosemarie's child.*

Isaac halted the buggy at the edge of the Miller's property, just by the low wooden fence and the little hinged gate that had been painted blue when Esther had last seen it. Now it was white like the fence, and the paint was peeling and faded. Esther climbed down from the buggy, conscious of her English dress, despite its simplicity. She didn't have her old plain dress to wear anymore. She'd thought she'd never return. But here she was.

The familiar sight of the old, whitewashed farmhouse brought a lump to her throat. There, by the side of the house, was the barn her parents had turned into a tailor's shop, where Esther had spent most of her time mending torn work clothing, reinforcing seams, adjusting hemlines and waistlines, and watching both of her parents fashion new clothes from plain bolts of cloth.

There were chickens running free in the yard, pecking at the ground, supervised by a young rooster strutting idly in their midst. Esther noticed what seemed to be old sewing machines recycled into benches and desks littering the lawn. Behind her, Isaac watched, a comforting, familiar presence.

She unlatched the little gate and walked in. Halfway down the narrow, gravel lined path to the front door, Esther heard a thump from inside the house and then the door flew open. Her mother stood in the doorway. The long dark ribbons of her bonnet fluttered as a gentle spring wind blew, carrying with it tiny, white petals, and the scent of apple blossoms.

"Essie!" her mother cried. Then she was running down the path to meet Esther and fold her into a warm embrace. "Oh, my child. You are back," she murmured into Esther hair.

Esther hugged her just as tightly. "I'm sorry." A movement in the doorway caught Esther's eye and she looked up to find her father and brother by the door, staring at her in shock. Then they too were running towards her, chickens scurrying out of their way with angry squawks.

She was home.

##

Isaac sat at the Millers' dining table, discreetly wiping at the little stain of drool his son had left on his dark waistcoat. At the Sunday service that morning, Esther had been baptized into the Church, with the entire congregation as witness. Afterwards, Anne Miller had invited Isaac and his entire family for a feast. She would be slaughtering and roasting three chickens, she'd said.

On the side of the table, Esther smiled at something her younger brother, Reuben, said. She was dressed in Amish plain garb again, her auburn hair wrapped in a white kapp. Baby Aaron slept in her arms, unusually complacent amid the noise of the gathering.

The Millers' dining room was packed with the both entire Miller family and the entire Beiler family, including Isaac's younger brother Jacob's pregnant wife, and his other younger brother's fiancee. And for some reason that Isaac didn't want to examine too closely, the Millers had also invited Judith Stoltzfus, who was now sitting next to him, listening attentively to Tailor Miller. Why had they seated Judith next to him? And Esther hadn't even so much as *glanced* in his direction all evening. Isaac tried not to sigh.

At the head of the table, Samuel Miller, or Tailor Miller as most of the town called him, read aloud a passage from the gospel of Luke, his voice rich and deep. "But the father said to his servants, 'Bring quickly the best robe, and put it on him, and put a ring on his hand, and shoes on his feet. And bring the fattened calf and kill it, and let us eat and celebrate. For this my son was dead, and is alive again; he was lost, and is found.' And they began to celebrate." Samuel looked up at the dinner table filled with guests, and then at Esther, who smiled. Anne reached across the table to grip Esther's hand.

"So let us celebrate," said Anne.

"Amen," everyone chorused. The three roasted chickens shone golden brown in the light of the gas lamps as Samuel began to carve.

When they had moved on to dessert, Judith leaned close and said, "It's so wonderful, isn't it? All this? The Beilers and the Millers are like one big family. It would be a blessing to be a part of it. Someday." She looked him in the eye and Isaac stared back at her, at a loss for words. How could he reply to something like that? Isaac flicked a glance across the table and caught Esther looking at them, but she quickly turned away to deflect baby Aaron's swinging fist from the dish of mashed potatoes.

Judith followed Isaac's gaze. "I heard the two of you used to court?" she said.

"Judith," he said. "Let's not talk of courting when my son's mother was alive just last winter."

Judith's eyes widened. "I'm sorry," she said. "I had thought that you. . .that I. . . I've been inconsiderate. Forgive me."

"It's nothing," said Isaac. He pushed his chair back quietly and stood up. "But please excuse me."

\#\#

Esther watched Isaac leave the room quietly. She expected Judith to follow him out but the other woman stayed in her seat, looking downcast. Did they have a disagreement?

Ever since she'd come home, Esther had been hearing about what a good match Isaac and Judith made. The gossip in the tailor's shop, among the older women, and some of the unmarried women, was subdued but still there. Even though the ministers preached against malicious or aimless gossip, in truth, bits of gossip was how the townspeople spread news around and kept in touch with the goings on. And the tailor's shop was a common gathering place for women in need of mending. The women told her all about how Isaac had been having so much trouble since Rosemarie died, taking care of his newborn, unable to work properly, especially since Isaac's mother was declining in health and couldn't help him. It might be early, they said, but Isaac needed the support of a wife. And Judith was hard-working, kind, and God-fearing. Then in low voices, they whispered: *and she's a beauty too*.

With all that talk in mind, Anne Miller had naturally seated Isaac and Judith together at the dinner table. Seeing how well the two of them looked, side by side, how perfect they were for each other, had made Esther's gut churn and her chest feel hollow. She couldn't look at them, so she kept her gaze fixed on her side of the table, focusing her attention on little Aaron fussing in her lap, on her parents, her brother, and the food on her plate.

What right did she have to feel like this, watching the two of them whisper to each other across the table like they were already a pair? Was she jealous? *Thou shalt not covet*, she thought. She'd just been baptized and already she was on the verge of breaking one of the Ten Commandments. What right did she have to covet Isaac when Esther had been the one to ruin their future together all those years ago? It was her wild impulse, her sinful desire to break the laws of the Lord, and then her anger at being spurned that night, that had led the two of them down different paths and brought them to this moment.

Baby Aaron looked up at her from her lap, his eyes bright, his chubby cheeks flushed, and his mouth rounding into a little o of delight. He babbled at her and Esther smiled back, though she couldn't help but glance out the window, over her father's shoulder. Isaac lingered somewhere out there, getting fresh air and brooding no doubt. Why he needed to brood, she had no idea. But the set of his shoulders when he had left the room, the way he tucked his hands into his trousers, told Esther he was in a bad mood and went out to cool himself off.

Esther felt a pair of eyes on her and looked up to find Judith staring at her across the table.

\#\#

Isaac leaned back against the trunk of an apple tree and stretched his legs out in front of him. The night air smelled like dew, grass, damp earth, and new blossoms. In the Miller's yard, the scents of spring mixed easily with the smell of chicken droppings and the faint whiff of hay and horse dung from the Beiler's stables across the fence.

Essie, he thought. As soon as she had arrived, she and baby Aaron had been nearly inseparable. The moment he brought Aaron and Esther within sight of each other, Aaron would reach out to her with his chubby arms, as if she were his true mother, and Esther would pluck his son from his grasp as if it was only natural that she would hold him. Seeing Esther with Isaac's son cradled in her arms awakened an old longing in him, so deep that it almost hurt to see them—to see *her* like that. With the baby in her arms, it was all too easy for him to imagine. . .

Isaac startled at the sudden weight of a baby on his lap. Aaron gurgled at him, fists waving. He twisted his head up to see Esther with her arms crossed and an exaggerated scowl on her face. "Ah," he said, "am I in trouble for something?"

"You left your son in my care without a word, so you could sit here and have all this," she spread her arms to indicate all of the outdoors, "open air to yourself?"

"Oh, I'm sorry," Isaac said. "I should be taking care of him, and yet I simply left him to you all evening. It was thoughtless and irresponsible of me."

She raised her eyebrows, looking taken aback. "I was half-joking. You don't need to take it so seriously. I was the one who keeps stealing your son without permission. He's just too precious."

"He is," Isaac said, looking down at Rosemarie's son. Aaron had inherited her large, slightly rounded blue eyes, and the dark hair that curled around his skull like a lady's kapp was hers too.

Esther dropped down to sit next to him, stretching out her legs in front of her in an unconscious mimicry of his own position. "I know you might not think of asking me for help, so. . ."

"Help?" said Isaac.

"Yes, so I'm volunteering to look after baby Aaron during the day, so you can go to work."

"What?" He whipped his head around to stare at her.

"You heard me," she said. She turned and met his gaze. Their faces were close enough that Isaac felt her warm breath on his cheek.

Casually, he leaned back on his elbow, placing a bit of extra space between them.

"Everyone is saying how it was a shame that you couldn't attend to their horses and cattle anymore," she said, looking down past the slope of the hill where the lights of their two houses were visible in the evening gloom. "While your brothers could fix some common illnesses among the horses, you're the one they call when things are really bad."

"Aren't you busy at the tailor's shop?" he said.

"It's easy enough to watch a baby while I sew."

"Alright then," said Isaac. "I can pay you to take care of him once I start earning again."

"Aw, shucks. Keep your money, idiot boy," Esther said with a laugh. "I can't be gracious and neighborly if I'm getting paid, can I?"

"Thank you," he said.

"Don't thank me," she said, looking away.

Was he imagining it? The way she had said that, the way she wouldn't meet his eyes—could she be feeling the same pang of regret he had felt before, when he had picked her up at the Old Philadelphia Pike and driven her home? The regret that they were now unrelated enough—unconnected by any bonds of obligation—to owe each other gratitude at every little thing?

Oh, Essie, he thought. He looked down at her hands, clasped on her lap, the fabric of her white apron bunched loosely in one fist. For a moment, he wanted to forget everything: the night that had torn them apart, his marriage to Rosemarie, his son, Essie's own past, whatever English life she lived in the outside, the child she probably lost. He wanted to throw it all away and just. . . He buried his hand in his pocket and cleared his throat.

He just wanted to hold her hand. In that moment.

##

Esther looked up from her work at the *ding* of the little bell over the shop door. It was Isaac's youngest brother, Seth.

"Hi Essie!" he said, his gaze flitting about the shop.

"Hello Seth," Esther said. "Did Isaac send you to pick up Aaron?"

From his crib, Baby Aaron threw the unused pincushion she'd given him to play with in the direction of the new visitor. It missed Seth by two feet, landing in a basket of scrap fabric sitting by the door.

"Whoa, is that how you treat your uncle, little man?" said Seth. Aaron squealed a laugh. Seth turned to Esther and scratched the back of his head sheepishly. "No, I'm actually looking for Isaac. I thought he'd be here around this time of the day, but I guess not."

"He might be here at any moment," she said, her foot pumping on the pedal of the sewing machine. It whirred as the needle stabbed at the cloth she fed into it in rapid time, leaving only a trail of tiny stitches behind. "There's been a lot of sick cows this month. So he's probably held up at one of the dairy farms. Why are you looking for him?"

"Oh, it's nothing important," said Seth. "But I fixed his buggy, so it's all ready to go now."

"You fixed his buggy?" Esther paused in her work, the whir of the machine sputtering off. She looked up at Seth. "You mean he left on foot? With all his tools and medicines?"

Seth scratched his head. "I guess so? I was busy working on the buggy so, I don't know. But maybe he hitched a ride with someone."

Esther looked at Baby Aaron, puttering about in his crib. "That makes sense," she said. "Do you want to take the baby now, or leave him with me?"

Seth looked at Baby Aaron, who giggled and waved at him. "I'll take him out for a walk. My work's done for the day and this wittle itty bitty man is calling me out for some bonding time!" he said, making funny faces at Aaron.

"Best if you just take him home and stay there," a voice said from behind Esther.

Annie Miller ducked through the partition leading into the Miller's living area and thumped her thick accounts book down onto a nearby worktable. "They're saying there's a big storm coming this evening. Maybe even a tornado." She groped around for a pencil in the drawer under the table.

"A storm?" said Esther.

"A tornado!" said Seth.

"Yes, Old Yoder from the village store said he heard the warning from the radio." Anne found her pencil, sat down and opened her accounts book. "A few of the firefighters from the Station even stopped by Farmer Fisher's Buggy Rides stand to ask him to spread the word about it to those who didn't have a radio or a phone. So you better just stay home. You don't wanna get caught outdoors if the storm hits."

It felt like a lead weight dropped in Esther's stomach and for a moment, some nameless fear grabbed a hold of her until she forgot to breathe. *Isaac*, she thought. *Isaac!*

"Esther?" Her mother gave her a worried look.

Esther turned and grabbed Seth by the front of his shirt. He stared down at her in shock.

"Where did he go?" she said.

"I don't know," said Seth.

Esther let go of Seth and shoved her way past him and out the door. She didn't hear them shouting at her to come back. She couldn't hear anything except her own pounding, frightened heart. *Where did he go?* Someone among the Beilers would know.

##

Isaac cradled his sprained wrist to his chest and slumped down beside a cluster of sodden dandelions. His clothes were soaked and rainwater dripped from his hair. He could only hope that his bag of tools was still dry, but looking down at the darkened leather briefcase, he knew the water had gone all the way through.

He should have taken his own horse Pharaoh, even without the buggy, but he knew the young mare, Adriana, hadn't been walked in a while so he thought it might be a good idea to walk her. Isaac sighed and tried to wiped the water from his eyes but it was no use, the rain just kept pouring. Pharaoh was steady enough that he wouldn't have bolted at the first crack of thunder and lightning.

But on the road home, it had suddenly begun to pour, and then thunder had boomed and the young chestnut mare panicked, throwing Isaac off his seat. Isaac had fallen on his wrist and for a moment, it had hurt so much he thought he had broken it. But now that he looked at it better, he could see it was probably just a sprain. He wasn't a human doctor.

But sprain or not, he needed to get home. Even though it was only late August, he felt himself begin to shiver under the onslaught of the rain and the strong gusts of wind. He held a hand up to shade his eyes and looked down either side of the little dirt road leading back to the town proper.

The Yoder's dairy farm had been rather far on the outskirts of town. It was almost smack in the middle between Bird-in-hand and Intercourse, but further out from the highway so the only ones who would pass by this dirt road would probably be the Yoder's farm hands and the milkmen on their daily run early in the morning. Isaac was out of luck. Nobody would be coming this way, not in this weather.

He rose slowly to his feet, one hand on the trunk of a nearby birch tree to steady himself. The downpour had turned the ground into slippery mud under his shoes. Isaac would have to find somewhere to sit the rain out. He squinted up at the sky, one hand shielding his eyes from the rain drops. Thunder crackled, lightning flashed, and then. . . the rain stopped. Isaac blinked and wiped the water off his face, looking around. It really wasn't raining anymore.

But in the sudden calm, he heard, approaching from a distance, a rumbling, howling, whirring noise. It was like nothing he had ever heard before. Then, through the tops of the trees, he saw it.

##

"Isaac!" Esther screamed, but the rain and the howl of the wind drowned out her voice. Under her, she felt Pharoah shiver and halt abruptly. She dug her heels into his sides but he tossed his head and danced to the side.

"Please," she said into his ear. "I need to find him." He flicked his ear back and shivered again, his skin rippling under her hand as he backed away. He tossed his head, the sudden movement ripping the reins from her hands. *I won't find Isaac on foot,* she thought. She'd cover less ground, and from her seat on a horse she could see further.

Esther grabbed at Pharaoh's mane just as the rain stopped. She bent her head to whisper into his neck. "The Lord is my shepherd, I shall not want. . ." Then she heard it. She looked up and *there* was the tornado at the edge of the horizon. It moved through the fields, uprooting lone trees, and taking everything in its path. The sound of the tornado reminded her of the whir of her sewing machine, the spool of thread spinning, the wheel turning, the thin needle stabbing down in a blur, and the way everything could go wrong so easily—the threads tangling, the needle drawing blood on her finger. . .

For a second, she stared at the approaching tornado, frozen. But then, as if from some distant place, she thought heard the sound of

a baby's wail, and a man's voice singing. *In der Stillen Einsamkeit. . .*
She took a deep breath and grabbed at the reins, coaxing Pharaoh off
the road, and hopefully out of the path of the tornado. He obeyed
readily when she kicked him to move, picking his way carefully through
a waist-high field of dog's fennel as if he agreed with her.

"Yea, though I walk through the valley of death," she shouted.
Behind her, the tornado howled. "I shall fear no evil, for thou art with
me." A stray gust of wind pushed at her and Pharaoh from the side, and
then something small and silver hit her arm, falling into her lap. She
picked it up. It was a hoof rasp. One of Isaac's regular tools. *Isaac was
here!* And then Pharaoh nearly stumbled over a leather briefcase on the
ground.

In front of her, the turfgrass flattened in the wind, and Esther saw
the old cottage, built under the lee of an overhanging rock cliff that
extended past the house like a bended arm, the little house tucked in its
crook. Smoke rose from the chimney.

She looked at the leather briefcase on the ground, the silver hoof
rasp in her hand, and the cottage in the distance. She spurred Pharaoh
forward.

He would have gone there to shelter.

##

She burst in the door like a dream, or perhaps like a storm, dripping and
wild-eyed. Her auburn hair hung half-undone from its usual coil; dark,
tangled clumps falling around her shoulders all the way to her waist.

From his seat, crouched by the fireplace, Isaac dropped the strip of
fabric he'd been wrapping around his wrist and stared at the sudden
apparition standing in the doorway.

"Essie?" he said.

"Idiot," she whispered, her eyes filling up with tears.

"It's Isaac, not idiot," he said, by reflex. He wasn't certain who
moved first, but before he knew it, they had wrapped themselves

around each other. She felt cold in his arms. Esther had been out in the storm while he had been warming himself by the fire. He rested his cheek on top of her head and, without thinking, combed his fingers over the wet, tangled strands of her hair.

"Even your hair is cold," he said.

Isaac felt her stiffen in his arms and, sensing that she was going to push him away, he let her go and stepped back, just far enough that they could look each other in the face. She gripped at her unbound hair and turned her gaze away.

"Didn't it begin like this?" she said. "That night we bundled, I knew you liked my hair a lot."

"Quite a lot," he said. Isaac remembered that night. The images were seared into his memory, half-painful and half-wonderful. The week after he had driven her home from the Sunday evening sing in his buggy for the first time, he had gone to her house and formally asked her parents for permission to spend a night there, bundling with Esther.

The bundling had gone well at first, the two of them talking and teasing each other like normal. But then Esther had wiggled around in her blankets and muttered that her braid was giving her a headache; she usually slept with her hair loose, she said. Then she unraveled her braid and spread her glossy auburn hair all over her white pillow and Isaac lost all speech.

"I've never apologized for trying to seduce you that night," she said.

"We were young," said Isaac.

"That's no excuse for what I did," she murmured. "To both of us."

He took her by the wrist and sat her down close to the fireplace. He held out his sprained wrist and the strip of fabric—the long sleeves he had ripped from his shirt—half-tied to it. "Can you wrap this for me?"

She ran cold hands over the inflamed and throbbing joint. "Is it broken?" Despite being a dressmaker's daughter, Esther had been adventurous enough that she had more experience with injuries than many of the boys Isaac knew, including his own brothers.

"You make a good ice pack," said Isaac. "And no, just a sprain."

He looked at her and said nothing as she took the ends of the fabric and unravelled it, undoing all of Isaac's previous work. Then she began re-wrapping from between his fingers, working her way up to his wrist.

"I didn't mean them," he said.

"Didn't mean what?" she mumbled distractedly.

"All the horrible things I said to you that night."

She stopped and looked up, wide eyes locking with his. Her cool fingers dug into his forearm.

"I wanted to do it too, that time," he said.

"I know," said Esther. "But that's not the point!"

"No, listen." Isaac looked down at where she supported his hand as she wrapped his wrist. He threaded their fingers together, wincing a little at the pain of moving his hand. "That night, I wanted to touch you so much. I wanted to do everything with you. Do you get it? *I felt the same way*. But then I panicked. Everything was too much. I was afraid it would ruin our future. Plunge us into a cursed union, unblessed by God."

Esther remained silent, staring down at their joined hands.

"Being the idiot I was, I took my fear out on you," said Isaac, "with cruel words. And when you left, I knew it was my fault, but it was too late to take back what I said."

"After I left," she said, finally looking up to meet his eyes. "I threw myself into the arms of a man because he was handsome and he charmed me and I lived with him for more than a year. He left me when I became pregnant. When I lost the baby, I knew it was my punishment."

Punishment? For some reason, Isaac didn't want her to think like that. He brought his other hand up to touch her cheek. "I regret that I drove you away," said Isaac. "But I can't regret having Aaron."

Esther closed her eyes and leaned into his palm ever so slightly.

"I regret that you lost your child," said Isaac softly, "and it might be selfish of me to think so, but how can it be a punishment if I have you here now? With me?"

Esther's brows furrowed for a moment. Then she opened her eyes and Isaac saw the same Essie he knew all those years ago. A girl free of sorrow and the tangled threads of guilt, with her future golden. She pressed a chaste, soft kiss to his lips and withdrew before he could blink. But he felt her smile with his lips, and then saw it with his own eyes. She smiled so freely that the corners of her eyes wrinkled. Behind her, the fire sparked and the wood crackled.

Even as the wind howled outside, here in this old, abandoned cottage with Esther, Isaac felt his bones warming.

"Well, we have no choice but to bundle together tonight," said Esther.

Isaac chuckled and then they threw their heads back and laughed together; a pair of old childhood friends, and a pair of courting lovers.

##

That night, they brought Pharaoh into the house and coaxed him to lie down because the one room cottage was too small for a prancing horse. Then they huddled beside him and slept. In the morning, they rode back home, Esther holding the reins because Isaac's wrist was sprained.

In the aftermath of the storm, the crisp, clean smell of the air and the tentative twittering of birds felt, to Esther, like a new beginning. Isaac sat behind her, his arm around her waist.

Then he began to hum a song she knew well. She laughed and sang with him, "In der Stillen Einsamkeit, Findest du mein lob bereit. . ."

9 798822 370386